DANNY ORLIS

AND

TROUBLE ON THE CIRCLE R RANCH

DANNY ORLIS

AND

TROUBLE ON THE CIRCLE R RANCH

BERNARD PALMER

Danny Orlis and Trouble on the Circle R Ranch
© 2024 by Bernard Palmer
All rights reserved. First edition 1968.
Second edition 2024.

Scripture quotations from The Authorized (King James) Version. Rights in the Authorized Version in the United Kingdom are vested in the Crown. Reproduced by permission of the Crown's patentee, Cambridge University Press.

Cover image: Adobe Firefly
Character illustrations: John Ball
Editor: Jon D. Fogdall

Aneko Press Youth

www.anekopress.com

Aneko Press, Life Sentence Publishing, and our logos are trademarks of Life Sentence Publishing, Inc.
203 E. Birch Street
P.O. Box 652
Abbotsford, WI 54405

JUVENILE FICTION / Religious / Christian / Action & Adventure
Paperback ISBN: 979-8-88936-046-9
eBook ISBN: 979-8-88936-047-6
10 9 8 7 6 5 4 3 2 1
Available where books are sold

CONTENTS

CHAPTER 1

STORMCLOUDS ARISE

It was quiet in the Circle R ranch house in southern Texas. The Davis triplets and their cousins had fed and watered the saddle horses and shortly after dark had gone wearily to bed, leaving Clarence and Carmen Roper alone. The dark, bright-eyed mother of Phil and Maria was knitting quietly and her husband, who sat in a straight-backed chair across the room, was staring at the carpet. There was a hard set to his chiseled face and his eyes narrowed.

"Carmen?"

She looked up, dropping her knitting to her lap. "Yes?"

"What's that religious broadcast the triplets are so intent on listening to?"

She frowned and shrugged her shoulders indifferently. "I didn't know they were crazy about listening to a religious broadcast. Why?"

A grin twisted his handsome face and died away. "Oh, they were out in the barn listening to it on the radio when I called them to supper tonight and it set me to thinking."

Carmen eyed him uneasily. For some unknown reason he became disturbed when anyone mentioned religion. His biting criticism had been even worse since her missionary sister, Rosalita, and her husband, Jerry, had been drowned when their dugout canoe capsized in the turbulent waters of a Guatemala river.

"Maybe it just happened to come on while they were listening to something else."

But he shook his head. His big hands were clenching and relaxing, as though in cadence to the swinging of some invisible pendulum. "That's what I thought at first," he said. "I couldn't imagine kids listening to that sort of stuff unless someone made them, but when I talked to them about it, they said they tried to listen to it every day."

Carmen picked up her knitting. "We can't expect anything else. I know Rosalita was my sister and all of that, but before she and Jerry died, they spoon-fed their kids on religion. It's a wonder they're as normal as they are."

Clarence got up and crossed the room to pick up a newspaper. "I didn't think too much about it when they first told me; I guess I didn't think listening to a religious broadcast meant anything. But now that I've got to thinking about it, I'm beginning to wonder just exactly what that program is all about." He went back to the chair and sat down. "Maybe you'd better listen to it tomorrow and see what it's like."

Carmen squirmed uncomfortably. "Why me?"

"If they've got our kids listening to junk like that, we'd better know it so we can do something about it."

"What do you mean?"

Clarence's voice rose angrily. "You know well enough what I mean. You know what Rosalita and Jerry were like – preaching at us every chance they got. If we'd have let them, they'd have made fanatics of both of us. I'm afraid those triplets are just like them."

Carmen gasped. "You don't think–."

"I do think they just might get hold of Phil and Marie if we aren't careful!" He expelled his breath with a rush. "If that happened, I think I'd find a hole and crawl into it. I'd never be able to hold my head up again."

When she and Clarence brought the triplets home to live with them after the death of her sister and her husband, Carmen had never once considered the possibility that one of their own children might be influenced to be religious. She had been looking forward to the day when she and Clarence would be able to influence DeeDee and Doug and Del to be more broadminded. The possibility Clarence voiced was staggering.

"What do you want me to do about it?" she asked. "Forbid them to listen to it?"

Clarence shook his head. "First, I think we'd better find out what the program's like. If it's just music, we won't have a lot to worry about."

Carmen smiled impishly. "Exactly why do you want me to listen to it, Clarence?" she teased. "You could listen to it yourself, you know."

"I might do just that. But in the meantime, I want you to listen enough to find out exactly what they preach. If they're as fanatical as that sister of yours, we'll have to do something."

* * *

In the boys' bedroom Phil picked up Del's New Testament and held it uneasily as though he was afraid it might hurt him if he lowered his guard for a moment.

"Does the Bible *really* say what that guy on the radio said it does?" he finally asked.

Del went over and sat on the chair near his cousin. "About what?" he asked.

Phil was having a difficult time saying what he wanted to say. He had never asked questions about the Bible until now and hadn't supposed it would be so hard. He could talk to Doug and Del about anything else and it didn't bother him, but now the sweat ringed his dark young face and he was trembling inside.

"About–about not being able to–to go to heaven unless you say you're a sinner and want Jesus to save you?"

"It sure does," Del replied firmly. "The Bible says, 'for the wages of sin is death, but the free gift of God is eternal life in Christ Jesus our Lord.' "

Phil sat down. Now that they had started to talk it was a bit easier. "I haven't been so bad."

"The Bible tells us that we've all been bad," Doug broke in, "and the verse Del quoted says the wages of sin is death. That means we all deserve to die."

Phil considered that quietly. It was different than what he had always thought.

"I figure all a guy has to do is the best he can and everything will be all right. That's what Dad told me."

"The Bible's got verses about that too," Del went on. "It says that salvation is the gift of God and we can't work and earn it. It says that if we could earn it, we'd get proud and boastful because we were Christians, and we're not supposed to do that."

Phil laid the Testament on the bed. "The only way we can get to heaven is to confess our sin and trust Jesus to save us."

Phil squirmed. "Dad would blow sky-high if he knew what we're talking about."

"Oh, I don't know," Doug broke in. "He didn't seem to be so mad when he caught us listening to that Christian broadcast."

"That's because he doesn't know what they say on it," Phil answered. "If he ever heard it himself, you'd find out what he'd have to say about it!"

With that, Phil decisively changed the subject.

* * *

Although Carmen Roper told her husband she would listen to the religious broadcast that the triplets seemed to find so interesting, she forgot to do so the next day. When Clarence found out, he was furious.

"Maybe you don't take this thing seriously," he stormed, "but I do. I saw what happened to Rosalita and that stupid husband of hers. They got more saint-happy every day."

Carmen's dark eyes flashed. "If you're so anxious to find out what's in that program, listen to it yourself. We've got three radios in the house and one in the pickup you're driving all the time. Don't keep harping at me about it!"

"If I want to find out what's in it, I suppose I'm going to have to listen to it myself. It doesn't sound as though you're going to."

He saw that the anger still glinted in her eyes. He came up behind her impulsively and put his arms around her. "I like to see you when you get a little mad," he said, his own anger ebbing. "You're the prettiest that way."

"I don't feel very pretty." She forcibly bit off the words and pulled away from him.

His grin was apologetic. "I'm sorry, Carmen," he said. "I didn't mean to lose my temper just now. It's just that I've been upset about having Rosalita's kids living here, for fear they might get Phil and Marie hooked on this religious kick of theirs. That would be terrible."

Carmen was as concerned as he was, but for the moment she chose to ignore her fears. "You don't have to worry about either of them getting religious." Her voice rose. "We haven't done such a poor job of raising them as all that. They both know better."

Clarence kissed her on the cheek.

"I hope you're right," he continued, "but I can't help remembering that's what your mother used to say about Rosalita when she first started going to that evangelical church. And look what happened."

Carmen winced. "You don't have to rub it in."

"All I'm saying is that we've got to face facts. Your mother didn't do that with Rosalita, and she not only went religious but married that hair-brained character who was going to convert the world – and look what happened to her."

Carmen nodded. The way Rosalita turned out was enough to cause anyone to think seriously about their kids. She wasn't going to have Phil and Marie get religious. That's all there was to it.

"I know," she admitted uneasily. "And it almost broke mother's heart when it happened."

"I'm thankful she didn't live long enough to know about Rosalita going off to Guatemala as a missionary and being drowned."

The hurt burned in Carmen's eyes. "You're not telling me anything I don't already know," she retorted irritably. "And I don't like it any better than you do."

Clarence's voice rose angrily. "Then do something

about it!" he snapped. "Find out what that radio program says so we can know whether to make the kids quit listening to it or not, and get the triplets away from their daily Bible reading. If you don't. Carmen, I'm warning you, we're going to have religious fanatics out of our own kids. Then we will have problems!"

Carmen looked at him, pleading for understanding. All Clarence said was true, she had to admit. Rosalita had been her own sister. She felt even worse about it than he did. But the triplets were so sweet and so very lonely. Just seeing them made her heart ache.

"I would do a lot more about it than I've done, Clarence," she told him softly, "but you know how much help DeeDee and the boys seem to get from their religion. It makes it easier for them to bear the loss of their parents. I'll take care of things, but I want to be careful that I don't have to hurt them any more than is absolutely necessary."

Her rancher-husband shook his head, unimpressed by her reasoning. "Well," he retorted darkly, "you'd just better not be too understanding. That's all I can say!"

She did not reply. It was a full minute before Clarence continued.

"I haven't minded having the kids here, Carmen. I think you know that. But I can tell you this much. If I'd known how religious they are, I'm not sure I'd even have agreed for us to take them." He sat down at the table. "They'd have been well taken care of by that Danny Orlis, or whatever his name was, and the kids would've loved it. They're as religious as Rosalita and Jerry ever thought of being."

"Clarence!" Horror marred Carmen's voice. "You can't be serious!"

"I've never been any more serious about anything in my life. It's no good bringing anyone into our home who's going to disrupt it. I don't care if they are your sister's family."

Carmen's face drained of color, leaving it a pasty white and tears trembled on her eyelashes. "You–you wouldn't send them away, would you?" she asked.

His grin came back crookedly. "Don't get so shaken up about it. I'm just telling you how I feel. I'd feel worse than you if the kids weren't living with us. And I don't think Phil and Marie would ever speak to me again." He grew serious once more. "The only thing that concerns me is Phil and Marie. I want to make sure they don't get to them with that religion of theirs."

There was a long, tortured silence. "You will listen to that program, won't you, Carmen?" he asked.

"I'll listen to it tomorrow."

"And if it's anything you think the kids shouldn't be hearing we'll put a stop to it. OK?"

"OK."

Some of the tension left the lanky rancher's bronzed face. "That's better. At least we'll know what they're listening to."

Still, Clarence Roper was strangely silent for the rest of the evening. Usually that was the time they talked over the happenings of the day and planned ahead, but he seemed strangely preoccupied. He sat down with a weekly news magazine for a time, trying to read. A few minutes later he switched on the radio for a moment, listened, and irritably snapped it off.

Carmen, too, was disturbed, but for a different reason. It didn't seem fair, somehow, to make the triplets give up their Bible reading and practicing the religion Rosalita and Jerry had taught them. And she knew it would not be what her sister would have wanted. Rosalita always said that her faith in Christ meant more to her than anything in all the world. She wouldn't want someone to forbid her children to practice the faith that meant so much to her and her husband.

On the other hand, Carmen could understand how Clarence felt about it. He didn't want Phil and Marie to be warped by a fanatical belief and maybe go traipsing off to some foreign country to be a missionary. He already had plans for Phil to go to work on the ranch with him, and he talked about Marie marrying someone close by so they could enjoy her and her family.

Carmen felt the same as Clarence about those things, and especially about not wanting Phil or Marie to go into some horrible place to live where they would be in danger all the time and she might never get to see them again. This was a much bigger problem than she had imagined it could be, and much more serious. She was obligated to Rosalita's kids, it was true, but her first obligation was to her own children and husband. She would have to listen to the religious broadcast the next day, and if it was like Clarence was afraid it was, they would have to forbid the children to listen to it.

The following morning DeeDee and Marie helped Carmen with the breakfast dishes while the boys did their chores. And, as soon as the work was done, the five of them raced to the barn and saddled their horses. Carmen stood in the window watching them, a smile wrinkling her face. It was so good to have DeeDee and her brothers with Marie and Phil. They got along so well together and had so much fun.

She was finishing the dusting in the living room when she stopped suddenly and went over to change radio stations.

Why she did so, she did not know. She had never made a practice of listening to the local religious broadcasting station. She wasn't even particularly interested in the program she had dialed. Then a beautiful, haunting melody floated through the speaker – a melody she hadn't heard since Rosalita and Jerry used to come to visit them.

She turned the volume louder and sat down to listen.

CHAPTER 2

CARMEN HEARS THE GOSPEL

Sitting alone in the living room of her luxurious new ranch home, Carmen Roper listened intently to the radio program. She was somewhat surprised to learn that the music she had found so intriguing was the theme song of the radio program that Clarence had caught the triplets and their own children listening to the day before. The program must be aired at different times during the day, she thought.

By this time, the choir was singing a second number, as beautiful as the first. Carmen adjusted the volume once more and scooted her chair a bit closer to the radio. She had always disliked such music intensely when Rosalita and Jerry came to visit and would happen to sing or hum around the house. More than once she had ordered them to be quiet.

And the lyrics! They stirred her heart in a way that it had not been stirred since she could remember. She found herself waiting eagerly for the speaker.

At last he came on, reading a passage of Scripture from the book of Romans. It was strange, she told herself, but he sounded exactly like Rosalita and Jerry. They were always talking about sin and the fact that every person was a sinner and had to be reconciled with God.

It had bothered her so much when they talked to her that she wasn't able to sleep at night and she thought she would go mad if they didn't stop it.

As the speaker continued, Carmen frowned her disapproval. She didn't know why he had to keep talking that way. She wasn't so bad. To hear him, he must think that people like her were criminals.

She shifted her position uneasily. She hadn't really committed any sins. At least she hadn't committed any real bad sins like breaking the Ten Commandments. She didn't even tell lies, except maybe a little white lie once in a while to protect herself or to keep from hurting somebody's feelings. She didn't even smoke or drink, and that was more than she could say for most of the ranchers' wives who were her neighbors.

The more she thought about it the more convinced she became that she wasn't a bad person. That speaker, whoever he was, didn't need to keep hammering at her as though she was the worst person in the world.

She tried the best she knew how to be a good mother. Everybody who knew her well would admit that. And she was concerned about religious instruction for her kids too. She had made arrangements for Phil to stay in town long enough to go through confirmation, and as soon as Marie was old enough, she would do the same with her. She probably would have to move into town herself and stay for that period, but she'd do that without complaint if it was necessary. She wanted her children to grow up to be good, loyal members of the church. And so did Clarence.

When it came to giving to the church, they both agreed on the importance of that too. They lived so far from town they weren't able to attend very often, but they gave regularly every year. When Clarence sold his cattle, one of the first things he did was to write a check to the church. And if she had lived close enough, she would have worked in the church as faithfully as her mother had.

Once Carmen had enumerated her virtues, she settled back in the chair, smiling. She was confident she had been living a good enough life so she could go to heaven without too much difficulty. She didn't see how anyone could do any more than she had.

But the speaker didn't talk as though the sort of life she had been leading was enough. He kept saying that every person in the whole world was a sinner and headed for hell unless he told God he was a sinner and trusted Christ to save him. Carmen scowled and would have switched off the radio at once, but something stopped her.

"For all have sinned, and fall short of the glory of God," the radio speaker intoned solemnly. "There is none righteous, not even one."

Carmen felt the color seep from her dark cheeks as the quiet voice drove its barbs into her heart. This wasn't the first time she had heard those same verses. Rosalita and her husband had quoted them several times when they talked with her about her relationship with God the last time they visited the ranch.

She could still remember her barbed reply, the hurt in Rosalita's tender face, and the sleepless night that followed. For several days those verses plagued her before she was able to shrug them off. She had not thought about them again until the night she received word that Rosalita and Jerry had drowned. Then a thought kept prying in at the edges of her mind, What if she and Clarence had been killed instead? Would they have gone to heaven? That, too, she had been able to thrust aside in time, but now it came flooding back.

The speaker continued quietly. "The time is coming when every knee is going to bow in homage to Christ. If you confess your sin and bow your will and heart to Him on this side of death, you will go to heaven. If you wait, you will be lost for all eternity."

Again, Carmen's temper surged through her being. There was more, but she wouldn't listen to it. He didn't have to talk to her that way. She was just as good as he was, even though she hadn't made a fanatic of herself like Rosalita. With a sudden gesture she switched off the radio.

Carmen started to get to her feet but stopped and settled back in the chair for a moment. Clarence was right. It wasn't safe for Phil and Marie to hear a program like that. The speaker was too forceful – what he said pierced her mind like an arrow. If they kept listening to him, they'd soon be as fanatical as DeeDee and her brothers, and she and Clarence would have a terrific problem on their hands.

The longer she sat there the angrier she became. At last she got up and attacked her housework furiously. Often work was a way of escape for her; when she had a special problem or was depressed about something she found that working hard helped her to forget. But this particular morning it seemed to make no difference: she vacuumed the rugs, waxed the kitchen floor, and rearranged the furniture in the living room but, regardless of how hard she worked, the ache in her heart continued to grow.

Sharp, penetrating pains hammered at the back of her head and at times her vision blurred. At last she could continue to work no longer. By the time Clarence came in for lunch at noon she was in bed with a migraine headache.

He made some coffee and fixed himself a couple of sandwiches and several for the kids to eat whenever they returned from riding their horses. And, before going out to work, he went into the bedroom and talked with Carmen briefly.

"Feel better now, Carmen?" he asked.

She opened her eyes. "I'm not sure."

"You'd better stay in bed this afternoon."

"I think I will. I feel terrible every time I get up."

He kissed her tenderly and started for the door. "Oh, yes, Carmen, in case you get to feeling better this afternoon, that radio program I've been wanting you to hear comes on at 5:30."

His dark-haired wife rubbed weakly at her forehead. She should tell him that she had already listened to the radio preacher. That was the reason she was in bed sick, but she didn't. If he knew about it, he would only ask questions and she didn't feel like answering them at the moment. So she told another of her little white lies.

"I don't think I feel like listening to anything this afternoon, let alone a religious program like that one must be."

The instant she spoke her conscience condemned her and brought to mind the Bible verses the radio preacher had been quoting. But it wasn't really a lie, she told herself doggedly. She didn't want to listen to the radio program that afternoon. She had a terrible headache and couldn't bear the thought of hearing the noise of the radio. But even as she tried to placate herself with such reasoning, she realized that she had been lying to him by intent. He wanted her to be able to tell him what the program was like, and she already knew. Only she couldn't bring herself to talk about it to Clarence or anyone.

"I can't say that I blame you," he replied. "I have a notion to make the kids stop listening to that program on general principles."

Carmen nodded but did not speak aloud. She agreed with him completely. If listening to a radio program could upset a person the way she was upset, what could it do to a couple of impressionable children like Phil and Marie?

She lay back and closed her eyes as her husband went out the door. She did not sleep, however. A portion of one of the Bible verses she heard that morning kept racing through her mind. "The wages of sin is death–the wages of sin is death–the wages of sin is death." She almost cried out in agony.

When Clarence came back to the ranch house that evening her headache was no better than it had been at noon. With the help of DeeDee and Marie he managed to get supper and the dishes done. Until bedtime he had everybody tiptoeing around and talking in whispers. She dozed now and again but was so restless and slept so light she was glad for Clarence's consideration. The next morning when she woke up her migraine was gone, but the uneasiness still remained, and the ache was still present in her heart.

Clarence had a job for the kids to do that day. "I want you to take a lunch with you," he said, "and ride the entire fence around the winter pasture."

Phil groaned. "Dad, that's a lot of riding. Can't we split it up? We could take care of half of it today and the other half in a day or two."

His dad would not change the arrangement. "Nope. I want you to cover the whole fence. We don't want to see you back here until suppertime."

Del and Doug grinned in anticipation. A job like that wasn't real work at all. There wasn't anything they got to do on the ranch that they enjoyed any more than riding anyway. It was great to be able to ride and actually do something for Uncle Clarence at the same time.

Phil glanced at the clouds and the stiffening northwest wind.

"It looks as though it's going to rain, Dad," he went on, a note of protest in his voice. "You don't mean that you want us to stay out if it starts to rain, do you?"

His father reached over and rumpled his dark hair good-naturedly. "Now, what kind of a dad do you think I am? No, I wouldn't want you to stay out if it starts to rain. In fact, I want you to come home, if it looks as though it's going to rain. It's just that your mother's been sick, and I thought it would be better if she could have another day of rest before you young scamps start kicking up a storm around the house."

A strange look clouded Marie's thin face. "Daddy!" she protested. "You talk as though we're little kids. We wouldn't be making enough noise to bother her."

His smile was warm and tender. It always was as far as Marie was concerned. "I just think it would be a little better if there's nobody around the house today," he explained. "Mother usually needs a lot of sleep after these bouts with migraine headaches."

The kids saddled their horses and rode along the fence at a brisk, distance-gobbling trot – the sort of pace a good cow pony could maintain mile after mile without tiring.

The sun was hidden briefly behind huge, rolling clouds that seemed to press lower with each passing hour until they appeared to be but a few scant yards above the crest of the hills that surrounded the Circle R. The wind whistled eerily through the mesquite and kicked up little puffs of dust here and there where the grass was thin. Although they were in southern Texas where it was usually very hot that time of year, the wind had a chill to it that made them wish they had brought along their jackets.

"I don't see why Dad didn't tell us to be quiet around the house today and let us do this when the weather's a little nicer," Phil complained.

"This isn't bad," Del retorted. "I sort of like it. It's exciting being out here on horseback actually doing something for your dad."

"You'll soon get over that. As far as I'm concerned there isn't much excitement to riding fence. Especially on a day like this."

Doug glanced up as though to check the time by the sun.

"I don't know about the rest of you, but I'm getting hungry."

"Want to stop here?"

DeeDee spoke up quickly. "We want to find a better place for our picnic than this." She looked about, wrinkling her nose distastefully. "There aren't even any trees."

Del glanced at the grotesquely twisted mesquite

that was scattered sparsely about them. The scrubby growth didn't look much like trees, for a fact.

"We're apt to have to ride all day to find anything that even looks like a tree," Del reminded her. "This isn't Guatemala, you know."

At the mention of the country where they had lived until their parents drowned, DeeDee flinched. The happiness faded momentarily from her eyes.

"We'll find some trees over the next hill," Phil said. "They aren't much for trees, but they're the best we've got right close, so they'll have to do."

There was a small creek on the other side of the hill and on the opposite bank a few scraggling willows and other trees the Davis boys didn't recognize stood in a small grove.

"You do have some trees out here," Doug said, swinging out of the saddle. "I thought you were kidding when you started talking about Texas trees."

"We've got trees," Phil countered. "Don't you forget it."

Marie stood in her stirrups. "I've seen better picnic places than this," she muttered.

"Not within ten miles of here, you haven't."

DeeDee's smile was contagious. "I think it's very nice."

Del dismounted and led his horse to the creek to drink. While he was doing so his brother turned to Phil. "Who'd ever plant trees way out here?"

"That used to bug me too. Dad says, though, that there used to be a homesteader up the creek a couple of miles. He was a nut on trees and planted them every-where before the drought came and he had to leave."

DeeDee's eyes brightened at the thought that there might be an old house nearby. "Are the old build-ings still there?"

"I guess so." He focused quizzically on her. "At least they were there the last time I went by the place. But why are you so interested in a bunch of old buildings? There's nothing in them but a bunch of junk and ten years' dust."

"I just love going through old houses," she said, shivering. "It's the most fun – even if I do get half scared to death when we do it."

Doug spoke up quickly. "Don't listen to her, Phil!

She's just trying to get you to say you'll take us over and see the old place, that's all. She'll get us hooked into a long ride for nothing."

Phil started to speak but stopped and eyed his attractive young cousin. "Maybe going over there wouldn't be such a bad idea, at that. I sort of get a kick out of going through old buildings myself."

DeeDee leaned forward excitedly. "Then you'll take us over there?" she demanded.

"If we get through riding fence in this end of the pasture early enough so we can go through the buildings and still be home before dark, we can," he told her. "Dad doesn't like to have us stay out after night. He says there are too many things that can happen after it gets dark."

DeeDee shivered again. "If you're thinking about old houses, don't talk about going through one after dark. I get positively petrified in the daytime. I wouldn't even be able to go near an empty house at night."

Del snorted his disgust. "Phil, did you ever hear anything so crazy?" he asked. "Old houses scare her silly, but she isn't happy until she's been through every vacant house within fifty miles of where she is." He shook his head. "I sure don't get it."

She made a little face at him. "The trouble with you is that you just don't understand."

"You can say that again."

After they finished eating lunch and let their horses graze and rest for a time they rode to the far end of the pasture, across the end, and started down the other side. It didn't take very long until they had ridden it all. Phil had not expected to find any breaks in it, but they did. There were two or three places where the wires were loose, however, and the top strand had been broken in one, probably by a steer rubbing against it. Del and Doug soon learned why Phil didn't particularly like to fix fence – it was hard work. By the time they finished fixing the last break, sweat was pouring down their cheeks in spite of the cold.

"Well," Phil said, "that's that. I think we'd better come out and get the other side tomorrow."

"I thought your dad wanted us to finish today," Del said.

"There's too much work to do to finish that today."

He grinned. "Dad wants the fence fixed, but the main reason he gave us so much to do was to be sure we wouldn't be back right after lunch to bother Mom."

"What about the old house?" DeeDee asked.

Phil reined in and looked from one face to another. "Well, what do you want to do? Do you want to go on home or go over and take a look at the old house?"

Doug glanced at the clouds. "What about the rain?"

"It hasn't started yet."

DeeDee spoke up quickly. "No, and I don't think it's going to. If we hurry, we can get over there and go through the old house and still get home before dark."

The boys looked at one another.

"What do you think?" Phil persisted.

"I sure don't care about getting wet," Del put in. "How about you, Doug?"

"I don't care much about getting wet either, but I know DeeDee likes to go through old houses."

Before Phil could speak there was a sudden rattling sound. Marie's horse squealed in terror and jumped to one side. Marie tried valiantly to hang on, but it was no use. She pitched headlong to the ground!

CHAPTER 3

MARIE'S ACCIDENT

The rattlesnake sounded again, suddenly shattering the taut silence.

Although already free of her rider, Marie's mount squealed in terror and shied once more at the fearful, startling sound. Then, with a great leap she bolted across the huge pasture, her silvery mane flying and her hooves thundering on the pavement-hard ground.

But the triplets and Phil heard nothing. Nor did they notice that the horse was running away. Marie was lying motionless on the sunbaked prairie! Marie, whose laughter had rung out only an instant before, was white and still, her lithe young body crumpled in a strangely grotesque position.

"Marie!" DeeDee cried almost involuntarily. For some reason, the accident robbed her legs of strength. She clung to the saddle horn woodenly. "Marie!"

They all stared down at her, too frightened to

move. Phil cried out in anguish. That seemed to free DeeDee to action. She swung off her pony, automatically dropping the reins as the boys did the same, and went running to the prostrate girl. Phil and her brothers were right behind her.

"Marie!" DeeDee cried again. "Are you alright?" She flung herself to the ground beside her injured cousin. "Are you alright?"

There was no sound except Marie's tortured breathing, and that was so light and feathery it was all but impossible to tell whether it was real or not.

By this time Phil reached his sister's side with Doug and Del half a step behind him. He dropped to his knees beside her and stared numbly at her limp form and sallow face. Her eyes were closed and there seemed to be no life in her body. He reached out impulsively to touch her but stopped uncertainly. His head swam and for a time he was afraid he was going to be sick. Marie was hurt. There was no way of knowing how bad. She–she might even be dead! A tortured groan escaped his lips.

"Marie!" His voice broke. "Marie!"

Del pushed closer, eyes widening.

"Is–is she hurt bad?" he asked, his voice so taut it scarcely sounded like his own.

Finally at the sound of Del's imploring voice her eyelids parted in a thin crack and she moaned oddly.

"She's alive!" Doug breathed. "We can thank God for that!"

Still, concern edged Phil's voice when he spoke.

"Marie!" he cried, panic seizing him. "Marie! Don't lie there so still! Answer me!"

She groaned again and, struggling, she opened her eyes a little wider.

"Marie!"

She stirred restlessly and blinked, as though she was just waking up from a sleep. Only it was different than that. Phil didn't know quite how, but it was different, and that difference struck fear into him.

She groaned once more and struggled to open her eyes a little wider. "Wh-what happened?" she murmured woodenly.

"You got thrown."

She shook her head. "No," she protested. "No, I didn't get thrown. Princess would never do a thing like that."

"You can't expect a horse to stand still when a snake rattles practically under her front feet," Phil told her.

Marie closed her eyes once more and it was some time before she was able to speak. "I knew it." In spite of her pain she smiled briefly. "I knew Princess wouldn't buck unless there was some very good reason."

"Are you alright?" DeeDee broke in.

But it was almost as though Marie didn't hear her. She continued to talk in that thin monotone.

"I wondered what happened. We were sitting there talking when all of a sudden Princess shied and threw me. But I knew she wouldn't do it on purpose."

"Are you hurt?" Phil asked.

Marie's lips trembled as she focused on him.

"I–I don't know for sure, Phil. I think it's my–."

She tried to move her left foot, but could only move it slightly.

DeeDee suddenly noticed how swollen Marie's ankle was. "Look!" she cried, pointing.

Phil gasped when he saw it. "I'll bet that hurts!" he cried.

Marie tried to speak, but for the moment she could not. Sweat was standing out on her face and forehead and her small hands were trembling violently.

"Do you hurt any place else?" DeeDee put in.

Marie shook her head.

"What I want to know," Del broke in, "is how are we going to get her back to the ranch?"

"I was wondering that same thing myself," her brother answered. "Do you think you feel able to ride, Marie?"

She replied hesitantly. "I–I can try."

"I don't see how she could ride with an ankle like that," Doug said. "It must hurt awful bad."

"I–I–." Marie stopped, looking from one to the other fearfully.

Phil's young face hardened, and when he spoke, he sounded exactly like his dad. There was even that same tone of gruffness that gave him a note of authority.

"She'll ride because she's got to," he blurted. "She can't stay out here!" He swallowed hard.

"But–."

Phil continued quickly. "We've got to get you home as quick as we can, Marie, so Dad can take you to town to the doctor."

She grimaced as the pain swept over her, but when she spoke her voice was firm and clear. She was a Roper too. There was a hardness in the family that seemed to be bred into those who lived in the ranch country – a certain toughness that made it possible for them to endure hardship and pain without complaining.

"I think I can ride if–if you can help me get on my horse."

It was only then that the kids realized Marie's saddle pony was gone.

"What happened to her horse?" Doug demanded.

Phil leaped to his feet and looked wildly about, but Princess was nowhere in sight. "She's gone!" he cried miserably. "She must've run away when that snake scared her."

"I remember now," Del said, his frown deepening. "I sat and watched her, but at the time I guess I didn't realize what was happening."

Doug turned to Phil. "Now, what do we do?"

There was a brief silence. Phil eyed the threatening clouds. If it had been earlier in the day and if it hadn't looked like rain, it would probably have been best for one of them to ride to the ranch as fast as he could to get Dad and the pickup while the others stayed with Marie. But it looked as though it was going to storm at any moment. And, even if it didn't storm soon, darkness was fast approaching. How would Dad find them in the dark? The trip would be hard for Marie, but about the only thing they could do was to put her on his horse and try to get her back to the ranch house before it started to rain.

"My horse'll ride double," Phil said aloud. "I'll take Marie with me."

Del held the reins while Phil and Doug carried Marie to Phil's horse and lifted her into the saddle. She swayed slightly and grasped the saddle horn with both hands. The boys grabbed frantically for her, but she shrugged them away.

"Don't worry about me," she said in a low, moaning tone. "I'll be all right."

"You don't look all right to me," her brother said. In spite of himself, his voice wore an edge of concern. "I thought you were going to fall."

She tried to answer him quickly, but started to sway in the saddle and had to grasp the horn again. "I'm OK," she said, "only you'll have to ride sort of slow. I still feel dizzy. I'm light-headed or something."

Phil swung himself up on his horse behind the saddle and took the reins. While he was doing that, the triplets mounted and they all started for the ranch house.

In the excitement, no one had noticed the clouds, but by now they had spread from horizon to horizon.

Thunder rolled ominously again and again as lightning knifed to the ground in great, jagged streaks that lit the sky. Doug turned in the saddle to watch it.

"It looks as though we're going to be getting wet any minute," he observed uneasily. He wasn't thinking of himself but of the injured girl in Phil's saddle.

Phil reined in and stared at the darkening western sky. There was no doubt that Doug was right about the storm. It had been moving up on them rapidly. Now it looked as though it was going to start raining before they had traveled another hundred yards.

"We're in for a bad storm," he exclaimed. "And it isn't going to be long getting here. We've got to get a move on!"

"Don't go too fast!" Marie managed between clenched teeth. "I–." She checked herself as her voice was drowned in a roll of thunder.

Concern flecked DeeDee's voice, though she tried desperately not to show it. "It wouldn't be very good for Marie to get wet," she said.

Phil's eyes grew even harder. There was desperation in them, but he spoke evenly. "We don't have any choice, DeeDee. There's nothing out here that will give us any shelter. We'll just have to travel as fast as we can."

Del spoke up. "What about that haunted house of DeeDee's? That isn't too far away, is it?"

Phil's eyes lit. "I never thought of that, but it is an idea. And it's only a mile or so over there. If we get a move on, maybe we can make it before the storm gets too bad." He looked at his sister who was sitting in the saddle in front of him. "Do you think you will be able to take some hard riding?"

"That's better than being caught out here in a storm," she retorted gamely.

"Good!"

They urged their horses to a brisk trot. In spite of the fact that Phil talked about hard riding he did not take the little group at a faster pace. Even that was too fast. He knew from the way Marie's lithe young body tensed that she was in great pain. He was glad that she did not complain. If she had, he didn't know what he would have done.

They rode for three or four minutes when a few drops of rain spattered down, increasing the chill of the already cold wind.

DeeDee turned to Marie. "Are you alright?" she asked.

"Don't worry about me. I'm getting along f-f-fine." But the tightness in her voice revealed the pain she was enduring.

DeeDee knew how Marie must feel, and she could not help admiring her. She went through the agony of her injured ankle without a word of protest.

The storm was moving rapidly and caught the kids when they were a quarter of a mile from the abandoned homestead. The wind roared down upon them, rain in its teeth, to drive through their clothes and soak them to the skin.

CHAPTER 4

PHIL'S DECISION

In the Circle R ranch house Clarence Roper was standing at the picture window watching the approaching storm with poorly concealed apprehension. He had sent the kids out that morning and had told them to be gone all day, but he hadn't thought they would stay so late with the weather as threatening as it was.

Wind and rain and lightning had never bothered him when he was out in them. He would hunch his back against the discomfort and ignore it as part of the price to pay for ranching. But it was different with kids. There was no knowing for sure what they would do or where they would try to hole up.

The lightning was one concern. It was particularly vicious in their area and claimed its share of livestock every year. The flash floods that would go roaring down the arroyos without warning were something else. And Phil might not remember about them, or might let the judgment of Del or Doug, who didn't know about such things, override his own. It wasn't likely that either catastrophe would overtake the youngsters, but this was a harsh country. One never knew.

Carmen came over and stood beside him, slipping her arm about his lean waist. She had lived with him long enough to know his every mood. He was concerned now, blaming himself that the kids weren't back yet.

"Do you think they'll make it back before the storm breaks?" she asked.

His eyes narrowed. "They should be back, but I couldn't bet on it. To tell you the truth, I thought they'd be back long before now." A note of self-incrimination crept into his voice. "I don't know what was the matter with me this morning, Carmen. I knew this storm was on the way. Even Phil saw it and asked about it, but I sent them out anyway."

"You told Phil to come back if it began to look as though it was going to rain, didn't you?" she asked. She was as concerned as he.

Clarence smiled reassuringly. "Sure, I did. And Phil is careful out on the range. You don't have to worry about the others as long as he's with them. He's spent so much time riding with the boys and me that he knows almost as much about taking care of himself as I do. He won't get into any trouble."

Carmen drew away, a wrinkle creasing her forehead. "I'm not too worried about Phil, or Marie either, for that matter. But Rosalita's kids know next to nothing about getting along in–in country like this. It's asking a lot of a boy Phil's age to take care of himself and all the others too."

Clarence stood motionless, as though trying to see beyond the horizon to the place where Phil and the kids were. When he spoke, he tried to hide his own nagging fears but only partially succeeded. "If they saw the clouds, they probably started home early. I'm sure they'll make it before it starts to rain."

Carmen drew in a deep breath. "It's not the getting wet that I'm thinking about," she said. "That's not going to hurt them much. But if they get cold and wet, they're apt to get careless in their rush to get back to the ranch. One of them might let a horse fall on him or–"

Her husband's lean face grew hard and there was an edge to his voice. "Now, don't go to borrowing trouble," he said sternly. "The kids can take care of themselves and all the worrying we do back here isn't going to help them any."

They were still standing in the window staring out at the lowering clouds when Marie's saddle horse came running up the lane and into the barn. Clarence jerked erect. His breath slammed out of him. Carmen's dark eyes widened, and her face went ashen.

"Clarence!" she cried, fear choking her voice. "That's Marie's horse! Something terrible has happened!"

He did not answer her. Instead, he whirled on his heel and made for the kitchen door.

"Where are you going, Clarence?" she shouted after him.

"Out to look for them!"

"I'm going along!"

He came back, briefly. "No, you'd better stay here. If they should come back on their own there should be someone here to take care of them!"

Carmen watched him go out the door and disappear in the direction of the barn. Her pulse pounded fiercely in her temples and her chest ached so, she could scarcely breathe.

Something had happened to Marie! That was the only explanation. Their daughter was lying someplace on the prairie, hurt. Otherwise, Phil would have caught her horse before she ran half a mile.

Time seemed to stop for Carmen, suspended by some invisible hand until each minute was an hour. Mechanically she went to the nearest chair and dropped heavily into it. She sat as though carved of marble, her eyes staring straight ahead, opened wide, but scarcely seeing. She did not even know when Clarence left the ranch buildings, and whether he went on horseback or in the pickup.

* * *

Once the Davis triplets and Phil got Marie to the abandoned house, the boys carried her carefully inside and laid her on the floor. DeeDee knelt beside her.

"How do you feel now?" she asked tenderly.

Marie had to struggle to force out the words. "I–I'm all right," she managed.

"Did riding over here make it hurt worse?"

"Well–." The injured girl spoke reluctantly. "It–it does hurt worse than it did before." She began to shiver. "But I'm all right. It's just that–."

"You're cold!" DeeDee exclaimed.

Phil, who had been looking about the building, turned to the Davis brothers. "There's an old stove in here," he said, "and plenty of broken furniture. If we only had some matches, We could start a fire so we could all get warm."

Doug quickly looked around. "There might be some matches in the kitchen," he said. "Some that got left here when the farmer moved out."

Phil disagreed. "We can look, but I don't think there would be any matches around here now. This place hasn't been used for years and years."

In spite of the logic of what his cousin said Doug went over to the cupboard and began to look through it. It soon became obvious that Phil had been right. When the farmer and his family moved out, they must have taken everything with them. If they didn't, someone else had come along later and cleaned up what was left, at least in the kitchen. There were a few broken dishes and an old glass or two, badly chipped at the top. In one of the drawers there was a knife handle and two forks with twisted tines, but that was all.

"You're right," he murmured, more to himself than to Phil. "I don't think we're going to find any matches in here."

The boys looked at each other with an air of mutual disappointment. Then Phil motioned them into the other room with a significant jerk of his head.

"I wanted to get you in here where the girls can't hear us talking," he whispered. "We've got a real problem to deal with."

"You can say that again."

"I've heard Dad talk about things like this. Marie must be in shock. That's why she's chilling the way she is."

Doug glanced apprehensively over his shoulder in the direction of the room where the injured girl was lying. "Is there anything we can do for her?" he asked.

"She's got to be kept warm, for one thing. If she keeps on chilling, it'll be even worse for her than it is now." As he spoke desperation gleamed in Phil's dark eyes. He had talked often with his dad about what to do in case of emergencies out on the prairie. He used to imagine what he would do if someone who was riding with him got thrown and broke a leg or something. He thought he knew exactly what to do, but now that they were actually faced with an emergency, he wasn't sure. He felt almost helpless.

"Just how are we going to keep Marie warm?" Del wanted to know. "Answer me that."

"Maybe there's an old quilt or some curtains or something like that in one of the other rooms."

Carefully the boys went through the rest of the dilapidated old house, opening doors and peering into rooms.

Phil couldn't understand it. Surely in a house where people had lived there would be something that could be used as a cover. Anything! But they found nothing.

Rain was leaking in through a score of holes in the roof and driving through the cracks in the boarded windows. It seemed that the only dry spot in the entire building was the place where Marie was lying. Uneasily, Phil and the Davis boys came back to where she was lying and looked down at her.

"How is she, DeeDee?" the injured girl's brother managed.

She felt Marie's feverish forehead. "She hasn't been complaining, but her forehead feels awful hot."

Phil's lips trembled and for an instant it looked as though he was about to cry. But he did not. When he spoke, his voice was steady. "The storm should be over before long. Then we can get her back to the ranch."

"Maybe we should try to make it back to the ranch," Del suggested. "We could leave now."

Phil would not agree to that.

"It's going to be dark in a few minutes, and in a storm like this, we could easily get confused and wander around all night, lost. And that would be worse for Marie than being here in the house, even though we don't have any heat."

"It would be a lot worse for Marie too," DeeDee said. "I don't think she would be able to stand it."

"But we've got to do something!" Doug blurted. "We can't let her lie there getting sicker and sicker without trying to get help for her. Let me go get Uncle Clarence."

"Even I might get lost in this storm," Phil replied. "Anyway, Princess didn't come back to us – that means she must have headed home. She'd get back before any of us could, and Dad's bound to know something's wrong. We'd better stay in the shelter."

DeeDee broke in quietly. "In all of the confusion, we haven't prayed. We should ask God to help us."

Phil snorted his disbelief. "You don't think that would do any good, do you?" he asked.

"Of course it will."

"I didn't notice that it helped your parents any." DeeDee winced but did not reply.

"You can pray about it, if you want to, but I'm not buying it. I'd a lot rather have a box of matches and some heavy blankets, or Dad, or a doctor."

The triplets eyed him solemnly, but they did not attempt to argue with him, in spite of the sneering remark he had made about their parents. It wouldn't do any good to talk with him about the will of God, and how He often worked in ways that men could not understand.

They could remember hearing their parents talking about how Uncle Clarence and Aunt Carmen had acted when they tried to testify to them about the

Lord Jesus Christ and to get them to see that they needed to have a personal relationship with Him. They had only lost their tempers and said things that hurt terribly. The trouble was, they did not understand. And neither did Phil.

So, instead of talking with him, they knelt and Doug began to pray aloud. He had learned to pray by listening to his parents; he didn't have a prayer memorized; he simply talked earnestly with God, the way he would talk to an old and trusted friend. He told Him about the situation in which they found themselves and that Marie was feverish and in shock. "We don't have anything to use to keep her warm," he said, "and we don't know what to do. Please help us!"

When he finished praying, Del prayed, and then it was DeeDee's turn. She started to cry a little as she prayed for Marie, but soon she was able to gain control of herself and continue.

Phil had remained quiet and motionless during the time of prayer but had not bowed his head. For a time after they finished, he looked from one to the other, as though he did not understand what had happened.

"Do you think your praying will do any good?" he asked, a note of seriousness mingled with scorn. "Do you think Marie is going to get well just because you've prayed?"

Doug hesitated. That was something that had bothered him a lot since the death of their parents. He knew they had prayed for their own safety as well as the work, but still God had taken them home to be with Him. It was enough to make a guy wonder whether it did any good to pray.

"The Bible tells us that God always answers the prayers of His children," Del replied. "He might not answer in the way we want Him to, but He answers."

Phil turned Del's firm, confident statement over in his mind. The very assurance his cousin had shown seemed to lend strength to what he said.

"But you aren't preachers or priests or anything."

"We're not preachers or priests," Del continued, "but we're Christians. And the Bible tells us that if believers ask anything in His name, He will do it."

That stopped Phil again. He looked beyond his sister at the door that was only partially keeping out the rain.

"You mean, if you ask for *anything,* God will give it to you? Just like that?" He snapped his fingers,

"It's got to be in accord with His will for our lives," Del continued. "And it's got to be in His time. God might not answer right away. He might have some reason for waiting. But He will answer. You can be sure of that."

Uneasily Phil crossed the floor, as though he didn't quite know what he was about. Then he came back to where Marie was lying, her eyes tightly closed, and looked down on her. It was a long time before he was able to speak at all.

"I wish I could be sure God is going to answer your prayers for Marie," he said, desperation growing in his voice. "I–I–." His voice trailed away.

DeeDee spoke quickly. "I'm sure He will, Phil," she said. "There's something else that we've been praying for and I know God is going to answer that prayer for us. So Marie *has* to get well."

Suspicion gleamed in Phil's eyes. "What's that?" he asked. "What have you been praying for that you know God is going to answer, but He hasn't yet?"

DeeDee squirmed uncomfortably. "I–I didn't mean to say that," she mumbled.

"What were you talking about?" he persisted.

Her gaze met his. "Promise you won't get mad at us."

"For cryin' out loud! I promise. Now tell me what you're talking about."

"We've been praying that you and Marie would accept Christ as your Savior, and she hasn't done it yet, so I know she's going to get all right."

Phil's cheeks paled. "That's the most stupid thing I've ever heard of."

"It isn't either," she countered. "We've been real worried about both of you, because you aren't Christians and if something happened to either of you, you'd be lost. You wouldn't go to heaven."

She paused, searching frantically for words. Phil was staring at her. He couldn't quite believe what she was saying. He couldn't understand why she would care whether he and Marie went to heaven, for one thing. And he couldn't understand what it meant to be lost.

He had been through confirmation and they talked about heaven and hell, but they had never seemed like real places to him. Not that the confirmation class had been told heaven and hell were not real places. Quite the contrary. The trouble was in his own thinking.

Del began to speak. "It's like the speaker said on the radio the other day. Everyone is a sinner. Nobody is good enough to go to heaven. It doesn't make any difference what we do, we can never be good enough to go to heaven."

Each word slapped Phil savagely, like a hand to the face. It seemed to him that he winced under the force of them. The hurt reflected in his eyes.

"If that's the case," he said, "if a guy can never be good enough to go to heaven, then what's he going to do to get there?" There was no scorn in his voice this time. Only deep concern.

"It wouldn't be possible for us to do anything if God hadn't sent the Lord Jesus Christ to die on the cross for us so we can put our trust in Him and be saved. But He did."

"I don't get it. I don't get it at all."

"So," Del continued, "all we have to do is to confess that we are sinners and put our trust in Christ to save us."

Phil filled his lungs with air and expelled it slowly. Several minutes passed before he spoke. "You make it sound simple."

"It is simple. A little kid can understand it."

There was another long silence.

"I've been watching the three of you ever since you came down to Texas to live with us after your mom and dad were drowned." He swallowed hard and it was apparent that he found it difficult to say what he felt he must. "And I–I know you've got something none of the rest of us have got. You're different than we are, that's all."

"If we are," DeeDee said, "it's because of Jesus. We're really no different than you are, except as He has changed us."

"Maybe," he answered, "and maybe not. All I know is that I could never live up to being a good Christian. There wouldn't be any use in trying."

"That's true," Doug said, speaking for the first time since they began to talk of spiritual things. "In fact, nobody can live up to it in his own strength."

Phil stared at him. "Then, what's the use of trying?"

"We shouldn't."

That surprised Phil. His lips parted in protest, but he did not speak.

"The Bible tells us that God will help us to live the way we should if we only trust Him. We don't have to do it alone."

Involuntarily Phil took half a step forward. "Do you really mean that?"

"It's not whether I mean it or not that makes any difference," Doug said. "God really means it. And that's the important thing. He tells us in His Word that he not only sent Jesus to die on the cross for your sin and mine. He sent the Holy Spirit to live in our hearts and guide us in the way He wants us to act, and in what He wants us to do."

For a minute or two their cousin remained silent. He was breathing rhythmically, but when he spoke his voice was taut with emotion. "I couldn't become a Christian," he said flatly.

The triplets stared at him. "Why not?"

"Dad would skin me alive if I did anything like that. He'd skin me alive!"

The Davis boys and DeeDee thought about that. Uncle Clarence did have quite a bad temper. They had seen him a time or two when he was angry, and they knew what Phil was talking about, but he didn't seem to be as bad as all that.

"After he found out you mean business, he wouldn't say anything," Del replied.

"You don't know him the way I do!" In his agitation Phil's voice rose. "When he gets mad – brrrrr! It's too bad for anyone who's crossed him."

The kids had been so intent in their conversation that they had all but forgotten that Marie was awake until she spoke.

"You can just know Dad would be mad if you became a Christian," she said. "You know how mad he used to get when Aunt Rosalita and Uncle Jerry would talk to him." She paused for emphasis. "I sure wouldn't want to be in your shoes if you do something like that, Phil! I can tell you that much right now!"

Phil glanced over at his sister quickly. What she said was true. It gave him the cold shivers just to think about his dad and what he would say if Phil told him he had taken a stand for Christ. Or, worse yet, if Marie or someone else told him. He knew the Davis boys wanted to keep talking to him, but he had to put a stop to it. He knew how close he was to doing what they suggested, and he didn't dare. He didn't dare!

Without saying any more Phil turned abruptly and walked away.

Del watched him go. He knew Phil was upset and he didn't want to put any pressure on him. In fact, he felt funny, as it was, because of the things he had said. But he couldn't stop now; he had to find out what his cousin was thinking. Slowly, he followed him into the other room. By this time, it was so dark they could scarcely make out each other. Rain was dripping through several holes in the roof and the chill wind was whistling through the cracks between the boards that covered the window openings.

Del did not speak until his cousin did so first. "What do you want?" There was belligerence in his voice.

"I just wanted to talk to you."

"I don't want to talk to you right now." The instant he spoke he was sorry. "I didn't mean that, Del. I'm sorry. I'm so mixed up I don't know what I am saying."

Del grinned. "I know a guy is supposed to honor his dad and do what he says. The Bible tells us we're supposed to do that. But this is one thing where I believe every person has the right to make up his own mind. He shouldn't even let his parents influence him."

Del spoke softly enough so the sound of the storm swallowed his voice and kept Marie from hearing what he was saying.

"You just don't know what Dad is like. He'd really give it to me if I became a Christian."

"Which is the most important," Del asked, "to accept Christ as your Savior and go to heaven, or do as your Dad wants you to and go to hell?"

The silence was long and painful. The only sound was that of Phil's heavy breathing. Del waited, praying in silence.

At last Phil spoke. "Tell me, Del, is–is that really true about God helping a guy to live the way he should? You mean, he honestly doesn't have to depend on himself?"

"If it wasn't, there wouldn't be any use for Doug and DeeDee and me even trying to be Christians. We couldn't live a Christian life for thirty minutes if we had to depend on ourselves."

But Phil was not yet satisfied. He lowered his voice to a whisper. "W-would God help me to face Dad?" he wanted to know.

"You can count on that. It will be rough facing your dad, but God will give you all the strength and courage you need."

The boy swallowed hard. "Believe me, I'll need plenty."

With that Phil dropped to his knees and made his decision for Christ.

CHAPTER 5

RESCUE

It wasn't raining when Clarence Roper left the house, but he picked up his slicker on the way out and wriggled into it. A few drops of rain began to fall as he ran across the yard to the Circle R barn and saddled his favorite cow pony.

The rain moved in with a sudden gust of wind, a driving downpour that rattled noisily on the roof and drummed against the glass in the small windows. But Clarence did not pause. He finished tightening the cinch and led his horse out into the stormy night. The rain stung his face and softened the ground underfoot as he tightened his grip on the reins and swung himself up on the big, rawboned quarter horse.

It wasn't good leaving Carmen at home crying and carrying on the way she probably would be. There should have been someone to stay with her. But it couldn't be helped. This was an emergency. There was no time to go over to one of the neighbors to get someone to be with her.

Marie's horse coming home without her could mean several things; perhaps she had been thrown and the other kids either couldn't catch her horse or were too excited to try. And if Marie had been thrown, she could be badly hurt; she might have been trampled or dragged. Whatever had happened it could be serious. He couldn't lose any time getting out to find her.

Ignoring the rain and the wind, the rancher rode down the lane, turned and headed for the far pasture where the kids had been riding fence. He kept his horse at a steady, long-stride trot.

Although he steeled himself against the possibilities of what could have happened to Marie, he was trembling inside, and it was all he could do to keep from forcing his cow horse to top speed. He might have to ride the powerful animal all night. He couldn't urge him to a gallop and keep him there, even a horse like General Joe had limitations.

All of this was his own fault, Clarence reasoned. He should never have sent those kids out so far with the weather threatening. He could just as well have asked them to be quiet when they were around the house until Carmen got up. If Marie was badly hurt, he had no one to blame but himself. He had caused it.

At first Clarence was hopeful that he might meet Phil and the triplets a short distance from the house. After all, they had been gone all day. They could have been almost home when Marie got into difficulty. He kept looking from one side to the other, trying to make out the figures of four horses and their riders in the rain.

But he saw nothing.

He had been gone from the ranch an hour or so when darkness came. Even that did not stop him. He kept his saddle horse slogging forward, doggedly, as fast as possible without sapping his strength. Every now and then he stopped and called out against the howling wind.

"Phil! Marie! Where are you? Where are you?"

But the wind hurled the words back in his teeth. He cried out again, trying to ignore the panic that was beginning to take hold of him. It was useless to call to them. The pasture encompassed more than a dozen square miles. The kids could be several miles away. And the storm was so fierce they wouldn't be able to hear him thirty feet from where he was.

General Joe, strong and tireless as he was, began to slow. Grimly Clarence urged the big horse forward. As he did so the chilling fingers of fear tightened their grip about his very being. The rancher was cold. He hunkered in the saddle, trying to forget his own misery. If it was bad for him, it would be doubly so for the kids. And especially for Marie if she had been injured.

It was not until he reached the rain-swollen creek an hour or so later that he remembered the abandoned farm buildings.

His spirits soared.

Why hadn't he thought of them before? Phil knew about them. He usually mentioned something about them whenever they rode in that area, and once in a while they stopped there. When the storm hit Phil undoubtedly took the kids over there to get out of the rain and cold. Marie could have done a poor job of tying her saddle horse and thus the animal had jerked free and come home. If they had decided to wait in the shelter until the storm passed, the kids might not even know she was gone. Clarence turned General Joe and rode in the direction of the dilapidated farm buildings.

When Clarence finally rode up to the ramshackle deserted house where the kids had taken refuge from the storm, they were all huddled in the living room in the dark. They were all chilled through and shivering, their clothes still wet, but nobody complained. They seldom said anything to each other, except to check on Marie.

DeeDee felt the injured girl's forehead once more. It was hot to the touch and seemed to be growing warmer. Marie stirred, indicating that she was still awake.

"How do you feel, Marie?" DeeDee asked.

Marie's voice was weak. "If–if I wasn't so cold, I–I think I'd feel a little–." She didn't finish what she was saying.

There was a sound outside, a different sound than they had heard since the wind and rain began.

"What was that?" The boys and DeeDee jerked upright, listening intently.

At that instant, the door flung open. It was so dark

they could not see anyone standing in the doorway. A board creaked beneath a heavy boot.

"Who's there?" Phil cried out.

"Phil! Is that you?"

"Dad!"

An instant later Clarence struck a match and held it high.

"Dad!" The boy's voice broke. "Dad! Am I ever glad to see you!"

"Are you alright?"

Clarence strode across the floor, moving close enough to see his daughter. "Marie!" He knelt quickly beside her. "Marie! What is it? What happened?"

At the sight of her dad, she began to whimper. On other occasions he had scolded her for crying, telling her that she had to be big and brave. This time he said nothing about it.

"There now." He felt her forehead, startled that it was so warm. "You're going to be all right." He turned to Phil. "How badly hurt is she?" he demanded. "How did it happen?"

Hurriedly Phil told him what had happened.

"Princess wouldn't have thrown me if that rattlesnake hadn't scared her," Marie protested. "Don't blame her for it, Dad."

He bent and kissed her on the cheek. "Don't you worry about Princess. We're not blaming her for anything."

Marie sighed. "I'm glad," she murmured. "I was afraid you or mother would make me get rid of her."

"You won't have to get rid of Princess unless you want to." He struck another match and examined her ankle carefully. It was swollen so terribly he didn't think anyone, even a doctor, could tell whether it was broken or sprained without an X ray.

Marie managed to speak between clenched teeth. "Is it–is it broken?"

He touched it again speculatively, but he did not answer her directly.

"You're going to be all right, my dear," he said at last. "In fact, you should be well in no time."

That seemed to satisfy her. If Phil or DeeDee or someone else had told her that, she wouldn't have paid any attention, but when Dad said it, she knew it was true. He never had told her anything that wasn't the truth. She closed her eyes and relaxed slightly.

Clarence got to his feet and went to the stove. They had to get the fire going and get Marie dry and warm. That was the first thing. Then he had to decide what to do about getting her back to the ranch and to town to the doctor.

"Boys, help me get some of this old furniture broken up," he said crisply. "We've got to get a fire in here right away and get the five of you warmed up."

Quickly the boys got to their feet and stumbled about the room, groping for pieces of old chairs and the table. In a couple of minutes Phil's dad had a good fire going.

He turned to Marie. "I'll try to be as careful as I can," he told her. "I'm going to move you closer to the fire so you can get warm."

She stifled a small, involuntary groan as he lifted her off the floor.

"You'll be warm in just a little while, honey," he said, his gruff voice tender.

The triplets and Phil moved closer to the fire at the same time. DeeDee extended her hands over the stove and rubbed them briskly. "I didn't notice how cold I really was until you got the fire going, Uncle Clarence," she said.

"I've been cold myself," he said, "and I had slicker on to keep me dry." He stepped up beside her. "It was a lucky thing for you that I came along when I did. You'd all have had pneumonia by morning."

Doug answered quickly. "We're sure glad you came along, Uncle Clarence," he said, "but it wasn't luck."

The tall rancher turned toward him. "And just exactly what do you mean by that?"

Phil was the one who answered. "He means that God answered our prayers."

For half a minute his dad glared at him in disbelief.

"What did you say, Phil?"

The boy caught the note of incredulity in his father's tone. Color sneaked up into his cheeks and sweat beaded his forehead. This was what he had been afraid of! He had spoken before he had thought and now his dad might find out everything!

"What did you say?" Clarence repeated.

"I–I said that God answered our prayers. We were so worried about Marie, and we asked God to help us."

Clarence Roper's face flushed beet red. Anger flashed from slitted eyes. "I thought that was what you said!" His voice rose. "You'd better explain some things to me, young man! And it had better be good!"

In the dim light of the stove the triplets could see the rage in their uncle's eyes. They had never seen him so angry before. They had never seen *anyone* so angry. Time seemed suspended as Clarence's angered gaze fixed on his son.

"Maybe you'd better spell it out, Phil," he said icily, "nice and slow, so I can understand what you're trying to say. Just exactly what do you mean?"

Phil's lips quivered and he moistened them uneasily with the tip of his tongue. He had known it would be this way when his dad found out. He had been stupid to think he could explain so his Dad would understand.

"I–." He stared up at his tall dad miserably. The words would not come.

"Speak up, boy! What's all this praying talk about?"

It was no use; his dad suspected something. He might as well tell him. "I–I was going to tell you, Dad," he began uncertainly, groping for words, "honestly, I was. But I thought it would be best to wait until we got home."

His dad's angered expression did not change. "What were you going to tell me that you thought you'd better wait to do until we got home?"

His son cleared his throat. "I–I decided to do something a little while ago – before you got here."

He all but wilted under his dad's steady gaze. "I accepted Christ as my S-S-S-Savior."

Clarence winced as though he had been slapped full in the face. Hurt drove the anger momentarily from his eyes. His arms dropped to his sides and the color seeped slowly from his bronzed cheeks, leaving him pale and shaken.

"You don't really mean that, Phil," he said in a dull monotone. "You don't really mean that–that you're a–a–religious–." Try as he would, he could not fit it into words.

Once the boy had begun to speak, he found it much easier. "I'm a Christian now, Dad," he said simply. "I've been wanting to be one ever since the kids came to live with us and–and I saw how different they were from me. But it wasn't until tonight that I really understood what it meant to–to get right with God and become a Christian."

Marie gasped audibly.

The triplets all began to pray for Phil silently. If anyone would need courage from God, it was Phil.

They could see the tension build as Clarence's disbelief gave way and he realized Phil meant what he said. An almost uncontrollable rage came over him; it twisted his handsome face, and the muscles in his right arm tightened as though he was about to slap Phil on the side of the head.

Marie, too, read her Dad's face and feared what he might do. "Don't hit him, Daddy!" she cried out.

Involuntarily the boy cringed.

Clarence relaxed a bit and took half a step backward as though to signify that he had no intention of striking his son. But the anger was still in his face; anger so violent it was almost akin to hate.

"He should be hit," he muttered. "My own son a religious fanatic! What I should do is take a belt to him!"

Softly the injured girl began to cry. DeeDee reached down and took her trembling hand. "It's all right, Marie," she said in a tone just above a whisper. "It's all right."

"I warned Phil that would happen," Marie murmured. "I warned him, but he wouldn't listen to me."

Clarence turned his attention to Phil. "Haven't I warned you about that stupid religion?" he demanded, cursing in a way none of them had ever heard him curse before. "Didn't I tell you that I wasn't having any kin of mine making a fool out of himself and me by becoming a religious fanatic?"

This time Phil did not waver. He spoke as clearly and as firmly as did his dad. "I know how you feel about it, Dad," he said, "and I–I'm sorry I had to go against your wishes. Honestly, I don't want to do something you don't want me to do."

His father broke in quickly. "If you really mean that, you'll forget all about this religion business."

"But I can't," Phil replied. He seemed to find strength in the act of speaking. The tremor had gone out of his voice and the color was back in his cheeks. Del and Doug saw that their cousin was not afraid anymore.

"I can't turn my back on Christ. I *had* to become a Christian. And I can't change my mind now."

Clarence remained motionless, staring fixedly at his son. Frustration and bewilderment and a certain helplessness mingled with the rage in his eyes. "You don't really mean it, Phil," he said, speaking defensively, as though Phil had to have his own actions explained to himself. "The triplets got you listening to those radio programs and then they probably talked with you so much, they got you all worked up emotionally. They tried to brainwash you. As soon as you've had time to think it over, you'll realize how stupid you've been."

His son's expression remained the same. "No, I won't, Dad. Nobody brainwashed me. I've been doing a lot of thinking the last few weeks – on my own. The triplets didn't push me into anything."

"You realize you'll be the laughingstock of the whole county if any of our friends find out about this, don't you? They'll all be laughing at you." Clarence smiled crookedly. "And do you want to know something else? They'll be laughing at me at the same time because my son's gone daft on religion. You wouldn't want that, would you?"

"I wouldn't want anyone to laugh at you," Phil acknowledged, "or at me, either."

"Then forget this crazy religion. I love you, Phil. And so does your mother. If there was anything to this religion you keep talking about, don't you think your mother and I would want you to believe it?"

"But couldn't there be something to it, Dad?" Phil protested seriously. "I mean – what the triplets said – it is all right in the Bible. I saw it myself."

The older man flushed crimson again. "If you don't stop that kind of talk, Phil, I'll beat it out of you!" He started suddenly for the door. "It's not raining so hard now. I think our storm is about over."

The kids listened. Sure enough, the wind had gone down until they could scarcely hear it. In the tension of Phil's quarrel with his father they had completely forgotten about the weather.

"Come on," Clarence ordered. "We've got to get back to the ranch and get the pickup out here so we can get Marie to town to the doctor."

Phil hung back.

"Come on, Phil! I don't want to have to tell you again!"

"I–I'm sorry. I didn't know you wanted me to go along."

"That's exactly what I want. You're going to have to go in the house and tell your mother what you just told me. I want her to see what kind of a son she's raised!"

CHAPTER 6

PRESSURE APPLIED

At home in Fairview Danny Orlis sat down in the living room and opened the latest letter from the triplets in Texas.

"It sounds as though they're having a big time, doesn't it?" he asked, scanning the first page.

Kay came to the kitchen door. "I'm sure they are. Most kids like it any place where there are horses to ride. And Clarence and Carmen do have the money to get them anything they need or think they need."

"But staying with the Ropers may not always be the best for them," Danny suggested. He read the letter once more, thoughtfully. "After what Jerry and Rosalita said about the Ropers, I guess we should have known, but it bothers me a little that they're getting some opposition to their faith."

Kay nodded. "I'm not surprised though. You could almost see the belligerence in Clarence Roper's eyes when he talked to us, and neither of us said a thing to him about the Lord."

Danny laughed quietly. "I guess he was afraid we were going to and wanted to serve notice that it wouldn't do us any good. He wasn't going to listen to us."

Kay took a step or two into the kitchen but turned back. "I have an uneasy feeling about all of this, Danny," she said. "The Ropers could make things awfully difficult for the triplets if they wanted to. The triplets might even begin to doubt their faith."

"That's what I've been thinking. We're going to have to make this a real matter of prayer."

* * *

Clarence Roper and Phil rode back to the ranch house on their saddle horses. On the way the rancher said nothing to his son. Even when they reached the house, he did not mention the angry scene at the deserted house.

"I'm going back after Marie in the pickup," he said. "The boys know their way back well enough to ride alone, don't they?"

"I hope so. They've been out in the pasture with me lots of times. Besides the sun will be coming up by the time they start back. They should be able to find their way in daylight."

"Good. I'll bring DeeDee and Marie with me and let Del and Doug lead the extra saddle horse."

By the time he reached the old house it was almost morning. Faint gray streaks of dawn were lighting the eastern horizon. The sun was completely up by the time they got back to the ranch house.

Carmen dashed out in the yard as soon as Clarence stopped the pickup, crying and talking at the same time as she tried to gather Marie into her arms.

"Take it easy, Carmen," her husband said, taking her by the arm and gently pulling her away. "Take it easy. She's going to be all right."

"I'm going to town with you," she announced firmly.

"You can be sure of that. Marie already has said she wants you along."

Before they left in the car Clarence called his son aside. "Just because I haven't done anything about this religion bit yet, Phil," he said, his voice ominous, "doesn't mean I'm not going to. You'll hear plenty from me when we get back."

The boy did not answer him.

DeeDee and her brothers came up beside Phil as the Roper car pulled out of the drive and headed up the long lane. It was a minute or two before either of them spoke.

"I'm sure glad Marie isn't hurt any worse than she is," DeeDee said. "She could have hurt her head or got kicked in the face or something a lot worse than an injured ankle."

Del turned to face his cousin. "What do you think your dad's going to do to you?" he asked. In spite of himself his fear showed through.

"He storms around a lot," Phil said, trying to mask his own concern, "but he's never beat me hard when I made him mad. I don't think he'll do a whole lot more than he's already done – except maybe take my radio so I can't listen to that radio program we've been hearing every day. At least, I hope that's all. Honestly, Del, I've never seen him so mad about anything before."

"I was as frightened as Marie was," DeeDee put in. "I thought he was so mad he was going to hit you with his fist when you told him that you're a Christian now."

Phil laughed. "I guess I was a little bit scared myself. But I don't think he would have done much more than give me a little swat or jerk me around. I'm really not at all afraid of him, as far as having him beat me up, I mean. He's not that kind of a dad."

The Davis triplets were visibly relieved, but Phil didn't feel any better. While it was true that his dad wouldn't do much physically to hurt him, there were a lot of other things he might do. Things that could hurt him even worse than a beating. In spite of that, however, there was a certain peace in his heart. He knew he had done the right thing.

* * *

Clarence said nothing to his wife about what had taken place with Phil until they got Marie to the hospital and the doctor had finished setting her ankle.

"You people had just as well go to the motel, Clarence," their family doctor said. "Marie will be sleeping for the next few hours."

"She'll be all right, won't she?"

"She's going to be fine. The break is actually in her leg just above her ankle. She'll have to wear a cast for a few weeks, but that's about the only inconvenience she'll have. In a couple of months she'll be as good as new. In fact, if you want to stick around for a day or so, you can take her home with you."

In the motel half an hour later Clarence asked Carmen if Phil had talked with her. "He was bothering me about something, but I told him to wait," she answered. "I was so upset about Marie I couldn't even think."

"Do you know what he was going to tell you?"

She shook her head.

Clarence's eyes flashed at the thought of what his son had told him. "Well, it's happened – the thing we were afraid of has happened."

"What do you mean?" she demanded fearfully. "Is there something wrong with Phil?"

"There's plenty wrong with him. Those brats of Rosalita's got to him!"

"What are you talking about?"

"It happened just the way I said it would. Phil's gone daft on religion. He's a fanatic! Just like Rosalita and Jerry and their kids!"

"Oh, no!"

"That's right! I tell you, Carmen, I wouldn't have believed it if he hadn't told me so with his own mouth!"

"But he–," her voice trailed away.

"It's those fanatical triplets who caused it," he continued. "This wouldn't have happened if we hadn't tried to be good and take them in. Look what they're doing to us after we've been so good to them! A fine way to repay us."

Carmen was as angry as her husband. "I'm going to talk to them as soon as we get home." Her voice rose decisively. "I'm going to forbid them to talk to either Marie or Philip about their religion. They won't say another word to them."

Clarence faced her. "If you'll remember, Carmen, this is what I told you I was afraid would happen when you wanted to take those kids in to live with us. And I told you it was the only thing I wouldn't stand for."

Fear crept into her eyes, and it was difficult for her to speak. "Wh–what do you mean?"

"I mean they're not going to stay with us anymore. That's all there is to it."

"But Clarence!"

"I'm going to call that children's home over in El Paso! We're not having those kids around any longer! If we do, they'll get hold of Marie too, and we'll lose both of our kids."

Tears clouded Carmen Roper's luminous black eyes and her lips trembled uncertainly. For a time, she looked as though she was going to cry. "I know how you feel about–about Phil," she said. "But I feel you just can't take your disappointment out on those children, Clarence. The triplets are Rosalita's children. We can't put them in a children's home."

Anger twisted his bronzed face and the words lashed out violently. "Oh, can't I?" His voice tightened. "And exactly what makes you think I can't? Answer me that!"

By this time, the tears trickled out from under her eyelids and down her cheeks. She made no attempt to wipe them away. "I *promised* that I'd look after them!"

He did not soften. "We have looked after them. We went up to Minnesota and got them and took them into our home. We've treated them the same as we have our own kids. And what happened?" He swore so savagely Carmen winced. "They've repaid us by getting Phil all messed up in this fanatical religion."

"He'll get over it." Hope trembled uncertainly in her voice. "You shouldn't let it get you so worked up, Clarence. It's just something new and different to him. In a couple of weeks he'll have had time to think it over and he'll probably be ashamed of himself for even thinking he'd want to be so–so religious."

That was the same argument Clarence had tried to make himself believe, but now he wasn't so sure. "I don't know whether you've seen that look in his eyes or not." He paced across the room and back again. "But I don't think he's going to change that easy. He looks and acts just like the rest of them." He paused and drew in a long breath. "I tell you, Carmen, when this story gets out, I'm going to be the laughingstock of the county."

"I don't think it's as bad as all of that."

"I do. And I ain't goin' to take any chances of it getting any worse. Those kids ain't stayin' here at the ranch anymore. That's final."

She went over to him hesitantly. "But Clarence!"

Belligerently, he swung around. "It's not goin' to do you any good to keep yellin' at me. I've made up my mind, Carmen. Those kids are gettin' out of here just as soon as I can get the children's home on the phone. And nothing you can say is going to change my mind."

Desperation gleamed in her eyes. "It's too late to do that now," she retorted. "The judge awarded the triplets to us legally. They're ours. We've got to keep them."

He sucked in a deep breath. "And just who says we've got to keep them? If a paper gave them to us, we'll get a paper to take them away! There's nothing so tough about that."

Carmen stopped crying. "I don't blame you for feeling the way you do about what happened, Clarence. And I don't like it any better than you do. But I know it's not going to last." She grasped his arm with both hands. "Let me talk to Phil about it before you do anything about sending the triplets away. Let me see what he has to say and how he feels about this religion after he's had a chance to think it over for a while." She paused for a moment. "Please!"

He stared down at her as cold and unrelenting as ever.

"Please give me a chance to talk to him before you send the triplets away. Please!"

He managed an icy smile. "If you're going to carry on that way, I suppose I'll have to," he agreed reluctantly. "But I can tell you right now. You're not going to be getting any place. And while you're fooling around, they might get next to Marie too. Don't forget that."

"I'll talk to Marie before we leave town. You won't have to worry about her."

"And another thing. Unless Phil does change his mind and forget this whole affair, the triplets go! That's all there is to it!"

She nodded miserably. She didn't know why Rosalita and her family had to go overboard on religion. She had grown to love DeeDee and the boys almost as much as her own children in the days since they had come to the ranch. She didn't want to give them up. And now, unless Phil changed his mind and said he wasn't going to have anything to do with that silly religion of theirs, they would have to go to a children's home. Clarence meant it when he said he wouldn't relent on that.

* * *

Carmen went into Marie's hospital room the next morning and sat by her bed to talk to her. She didn't know exactly how she was going to open the subject, but her daughter solved that for her.

"Mother," she began almost immediately, "what did Daddy decide to do about Phil?"

"What do you mean?" Carmen countered.

"Didn't he tell you what Phil did?" There was a tone of awe in her voice. "He became a Christian just like DeeDee and the boys."

Her mother nodded. "That is what I wanted to talk with you about this morning."

She told Marie how upset her dad was and how he was insisting that DeeDee and the boys be sent to a children's home because of what happened. Marie started to cry softly when she heard that. She had always wanted a sister and now that she had gotten one, she was afraid that she would lose her.

"You can't blame Daddy for being disturbed," her mother went on. "He doesn't want you and Phil to be the laughingstock of all our friends. And he especially doesn't want you to do what Phil has done."

"You won't have to worry about that," Marie said quickly. "I'm not going to." She smiled confidently. "I want to be just like you and Daddy."

"I knew we could count on you." Carmen reached over and patted her daughter confidently on the arm. "And when I talk with Phil, I'm sure he'll see how foolish he has been and forget this crazy religion of his."

"Maybe if that happens Daddy won't send the triplets away," Marie said.

"He's already promised that."

"If you tell Phil about *that,* I'm sure he'll forget."

Once they were back at the Circle R ranch house Carmen called her son, Phil, to one side.

"I want to talk to you, Phil," she said quietly.

He eyed her, questions flickering in his gaze. "Yes?"

"Come in here where the others can't hear us," she said.

Dutifully, he followed her into the bedroom and closed the door behind them. His mother sat down on a chair near the bed. She was not having an easy time finding words for what she wanted to say.

"Daddy is very angry that you–that you–" Her voice choked until she could not go on.

"I know." The clear, firm ring in his voice was disconcerting to her. Somehow, she had expected him to be on the defensive. She thought he would be surprised that she knew, and very much upset about it.

"We know that you–you like Doug and Del so much that you–you let them influence you into doing something that you don't understand," she said, "and that you really didn't want to do. Daddy and I both know that you–you don't really believe the way you say you do."

"But I do understand, Mother," he replied. "I understood that I was a sinner and wasn't going to heaven until I confessed my sin and–and put my trust in Jesus to save me."

She flinched as though he had struck her in the face with his open hand.

"But Phil!" she cried. "You went through confirmation! You have *our* church! You do not need another church to–to be a Christian."

"It's not the church, Mom. How could a bunch of people save me when they're as human as I am? It's the Lord Jesus Christ who saves."

Her anguish was deep. It was a full minute before she could reply and when she could, her voice was so strange she scarcely recognized it as her own. It sounded to her as though someone else was speaking – this couldn't be happening to her family!

"When you've had time to think it over, Phil," she croaked, "you won't be so–so fanatical."

Her opposition gave every evidence of strengthening his own resolve. Instead of listening to her and telling her he would think over what she was saying and try to figure out for himself if he had been wrong or not, he stood firm. It seemed to her that he was proud of what he believed.

"I am a Christian, Mom," he repeated with a finality that settled the matter. "I think I did the right thing."

She swallowed hard. Clarence had warned her, but she had not expected to meet such determination – such firmness of intent, especially from just a boy. Philip talked as though nothing could change him from the course he had chosen.

"Daddy is very angry," she told him.

"I know. He's already talked with me about it – a couple of times."

"He says that if you don't change your mind, Phil, and cut out this religious nonsense, he's going to make the triplets go to a children's home somewhere." She eyed him narrowly. "You wouldn't want that, would you?"

The boy jerked erect and his thin face paled. "C-could he do that?" For the first time his manner changed.

She nodded. "He not only could do that, but unless you change back to–to our church, he's going to hire a lawyer and fix it so that DeeDee and the boys have to go to a children's home."

"But why?"

"I've never seen him so angry since we've been married. He says he's not going to have any of his family going off the deep end on religion. He's not raising any fanatics! According to him, the kids caused you to go in for this–this foolishness. So he's going to get rid of them."

Phil studied her incredulously. "He wouldn't *really* do that, would he?"

"I'm afraid he would."

Phil wiped his hand nervously over his face. "Can't you talk to him? Can't you make him see that isn't the thing to do? I'm the one who went against his wishes. Not them. I'm the one he should punish."

"He figures this wouldn't have happened if the triplets hadn't come to live with us." Carmen paused. The conversation hadn't gone at all the way she wanted it to go. She had thought that Phil would see that he had done a foolish thing as soon as she explained things to him. But she had been forced into threatening her son, and she felt terribly guilty about becoming a partner in Clarence's ugly tactics. "I've tried to talk him into letting them stay, but it hasn't done any good," she rationalized. "There's only one thing that would cause him to change his mind about it."

"What's that?" Hope glimmered momentarily.

"Tell him that you've given up this religion business. Tell him that you've made up your mind that you aren't going to be a fanatic like the triplets are. That would fix everything. Dad loves the triplets. He is as anxious as we are to have them stay. It's just that he is so angry about what you have done."

The boy's eyes darkened. "That would be like turning my back on Christ, Mom," he said.

Carmen hesitated. She had always urged her children to tell the truth, but now she was so upset that she asked Phil to deceive his father.

"You could tell Daddy that you had changed your mind, couldn't you?" she suggested.

He stared at her. "I don't know what you mean."

"You could act as though this religion doesn't really mean anything to you, whether it does or not. Then, when you get older – maybe even when Dad has cooled off – you could go back to it. Nobody would say a word."

"I still don't understand."

"Don't you see? That would make it possible for the triplets to stay with us."

Phil shook his head miserably. His mom was a good person; she had taught him to never lie. Now she was urging him to be dishonest.

"I can't do that, Mom." His anguish was genuine.

CHAPTER 7

BACK TO FAIRVIEW

Danny and Kay Orlis had finished with Bible club that evening. The kids had all gone home and he was helping her with the refreshment dishes when the phone rang. Danny answered it.

"Yes, this is Danny Orlis," he said. "Yes. I'm sorry, I can't understand you. Yes, Mrs. Roper."

Curiosity aroused, Kay came over and stood beside him.

"Would you please repeat what you just said, Mrs. Roper. I can't understand you."

After what seemed to be half an hour to Kay, he put his phone down and turned slowly. "That's strange," he murmured.

"What was it?" Kay asked. "Is there something wrong with the triplets?"

"No," he answered. "At least I don't think there is. Mrs. Roper was very upset and crying so I could hardly understand what she was saying."

"What did she want?"

"I'm not even sure about that. All I could make out was that she's flying to Minneapolis tomorrow afternoon and wants us to meet her."

Kay put her hand to her face in surprise. It was strange that she was coming all the way from southern Texas to see them. It was very strange.

"And I thought she said something about having the triplets along," Danny continued. "I just can't figure it out."

"Do you think you ought to phone back?" Kay asked. "If you could get to talk to Clarence, you could get more satisfaction. Carmen is so excitable."

Danny considered phoning back to Texas but decided against it. After all, Carmen hadn't said the triplets were ill. They couldn't have been and still make the trip north with her. It seemed best to wait until they arrived.

The following morning Danny and Kay got up early and drove to the Twin Cities' airport to pick up Carmen Roper and the triplets. There was a distant, pensive look in Kay's eyes as her young husband pulled away from the gas pump and headed toward the highway. Danny noticed it almost immediately.

"What are you so quiet about this morning, Kay?" he asked.

She turned to face him. "I was thinking about that phone call from Carmen last night. It still bothers me." She paused momentarily. "What do you suppose happened that would cause her to call us that way?"

He shrugged. "I've been trying to figure it out, too. It's really hard to say. You know how excitable she is."

"But she acted so strangely."

"I know, but I wouldn't get upset until we get to see and talk to her."

"It must be something terribly important or she wouldn't bring the triplets all this way," Kay said, the corners of her mouth tightening. "They should be in school. At least classes started in Fairview last Monday."

Danny glanced at his watch. "I don't mind admitting it's got me puzzled, and a little concerned. But we'll soon know. They're due at Minneapolis on the 1:35 plane."

They got to the airport a few minutes before plane time and were waiting in the terminal when Carmen and the triplets entered. Danny spotted Carmen Roper when she was some distance away. Her walk was slow, each move revealing her dejection. Her shoulders sagged and her gaze was lowered. As soon as she got close enough, he saw that her eyes were red and dark semicircles were beneath them.

As she saw Danny and Kay, she managed a faint smile. "Hello." She held out a slender bronze hand. "How are you?"

"It's good to see you," Danny said.

Kay put her arms about Carmen and the dark-haired traveler choked back a sob.

Doug's eyes met Danny's. "Boy, it's good to see you," he said.

DeeDee and Del nodded emphatically.

Kay and Carmen went over and sat down while Danny and the triplets went to the floor below to get their luggage. Carmen acted as though she wanted to speak, but for some reason she could not. She looked at Kay with large, luminous eyes and started to cry. Kay put her arms about her, and for a moment or two, she held her close.

Carmen fought to regain control of herself. At last she was able to stop crying. "I'm sorry," she stammered, "I don't know what's the matter with me."

"Would you like to tell me about it?"

Her lips parted, but no sound came.

"We've been so concerned since your call last night, Carmen," Kay continued. "We couldn't figure out what could possibly bring you and the triplets this far, and such a short time after they went to live with you."

The other woman's eyes flooded with tears once more, and for an instant it appeared that she was going to start to cry again. She struggled for composure.

"We were afraid there was something wrong with the triplets."

"There is something wrong." She swallowed the lump in her throat. "There's something terribly wrong, Kay. And I can't do anything about it."

Kay's voice was soft and gentle. "Is there something Danny and I can do to help?"

Carmen raised her head to stare helplessly at her.

"I wish there was. But I don't know whether there's anything anyone can do to help – at least to solve the problem in the way I want it solved." She would have continued, but Danny and the kids were just stepping off the escalator and heading in their direction. Unheeded, a tear slipped past her eyelid and trickled down her cheek.

Kay reached over and patted her hand reassuringly. At that moment Danny stopped before them. DeeDee was on one side and the boys on the other.

"The kids said this is all the luggage you have, Carmen."

She nodded wordlessly and got to her feet. "I'm not going to need a great deal," she said. "I–I can't stay very long."

They left the terminal and walked halfway across the parking lot to the Orlis car in complete silence. Once or twice on the way home Danny acted as though he was about to question Carmen, but Kay stopped him with a knowing glance. It was not until they got back to Fairview that they had a chance to talk to her. First, Carmen sent the triplets outside in spite of their protests.

"We don't want to go out and do anything," DeeDee's voice rose. "We haven't seen Danny and Kay for a long time. We want to talk to them."

"You can talk to them tomorrow, DeeDee."

"But–," the girl protested.

"Do as I say." Carmen's voice grew stern. "Now, scoot, or I'll put you on time out."

Reluctantly DeeDee and her brothers left the house. Carmen watched them in silence until they disappeared from view. When she turned back to Danny and Kay, tears were trickling unashamedly down her cheeks.

"They don't really want to visit with you," she exclaimed lamely. "They are as upset and as concerned as I am. They're wondering what's going to happen."

"What do you mean?" Danny asked.

She did not answer him directly. "This is the hardest thing I have ever had to do in all my life," she said. In her anguish her Spanish accent thickened noticeably. "When Rosalita died, I was so glad that Clarence and I could take the triplets. We felt that it was the last gift we could give her."

She started to sob once more, so violently that her entire body shook. Kay went over and tenderly put her arm about her.

"Come on over and sit down, Carmen, and tell us all about it."

Mechanically their visitor did as she was told. For several minutes she cried so hard she was unable to speak. However, the crying seemed to release the tension and gradually she began to grow calm. At last she raised her head and wiped the tears away. For a minute or so she looked from one to the other as though uncertain what to say or where to begin. At last Danny spoke up.

"Would you like to tell us about it?" he asked gently. "Sometimes it helps just to talk things out."

"I don't want to do this. Believe me! But there's no other way!"

Briefly she started to cry again, but it was only a moment or two before she was able to check the tears enough so she could tell them what had happened. Danny and Kay listened without comment until she had finished.

"So," she concluded, "instead of letting Clarence put the triplets in an–an institution, I brought them up to you."

Danny and Kay both stared at her incredulously.

"You–you mean you and Clarence want us to take the triplets?" Danny asked. He could scarcely believe he was hearing her correctly.

"You will, won't you?"

He hesitated.

This was something Carmen had not anticipated. She had been so sure that they would take in Rosalita's children. New concern flashed in her eyes. "Won't you?"

When Danny answered his voice was soft and thoughtful. "You can't be serious."

"I only wish I weren't." She faltered momentarily. "I want to keep the triplets, but there just isn't any way of doing so. Clarence won't hear to it."

"Don't you think he'll change his mind when he gets a chance to think it over?" Kay asked.

"You don't know how upset he is."

"But you wrote how happy he was to have DeeDee and the boys live with you, and how happy your own children were. I'm sure that he'll be anxious to have the triplets back after a little time has passed."

Carmen shook her head. "You don't know him like I do." She shuddered. "He was angry enough when Rosalita married a–a Christian. He would hardly treat her civilly after that. And I don't think he ever sat down voluntarily and visited with Jerry in his life. I know he thoroughly detested him. You've never met anyone as bitter and antagonistic toward religion as Clarence is."

"He wanted the triplets to come and live with you, didn't he?"

Carmen shook her head. "He didn't mind having them, but he was afraid they would talk to one of our kids and get them twisted up in their thinking. He said that even if they didn't get hold of Phil or Marie, they would grow up to be like Jerry and he didn't want anything around him that would remind him of–of 'that fanatical religion,' as he called it. I had to plead with him to get him to let them come to live with us."

"I see," Kay murmured.

"After they came, he got to liking them and everything would have been all right if Phil hadn't decided that he wanted to be a Christian and told Clarence about it."

She caught her breath sharply. "You should have heard Clarence. No, he's not going to change his mind about anything that has to do with them. He said that if you don't take them, they've got to go into a childcare place in El Paso or San Antonio."

She started to cry once more. "It–it's hard enough to have to give up my own sister's children. I–I don't think I could stand it if they had to go into some public home like that. I didn't approve of Rosalita's religion either, but she was still my sister."

Kay patted her on the shoulder and said in low tones, "I know that what you say about Clarence is probably true, but I know that he's a good man and he does love you. When he realizes how much the triplets mean to you, he'll change his mind."

But Carmen was not convinced. "You've never seen anyone so angry!"

Danny spoke up. "Do you think it would do any good if I talked to him?"

"Oh, no!" she retorted quickly. "It wouldn't do any good for anyone to talk to him. He isn't going to change his mind. I know that. If I thought there was any other way, I wouldn't have come up here with the triplets." Her tone changed to pleading. "You'll take them, won't you?"

Danny paused. This was not a decision to be made quickly. It was something he and Kay would have to talk over and pray about.

"We can't give you an answer right now, Carmen. We've got to talk it over first."

Fear gleamed in their guest's eyes.

CHAPTER 8

SEEKING A SOLUTION

Danny and Kay Orlis sat in the living room that night a long while after the triplets and Carmen had gone to their rooms, talking about the decision that faced them.

"What do you think, Kay?" Danny asked at last. "Should we take them into our home or not?"

A smile tugged the corners of her mouth upward. "I love all three of them," she said.

"So do I."

Her smile disappeared and a frown creased her forehead. "I would love to take them, Danny. You know that. But I don't know whether I could stand it or not."

"What do you mean?"

"I've been thinking about how terrible I felt after Kent and Jill were taken from us," she explained. "I'm afraid we'd only have them for a few months and would get to loving them even more than we do now, when Clarence Roper would change his mind and take them away from us." The old hurt came rushing back. "I don't think I could stand that again, Danny."

He nodded pensively. "I know just what you mean. I've been thinking about the same thing myself."

"It isn't that I don't want to take them."

"I'm sure you do," he said smiling. "I've lived with you long enough to know that you're a sucker for any homeless kitten or pup in the neighborhood, and an absolute pushover when it comes to homeless kids."

"I know I sound terribly selfish, Danny." Tears came to her eyes. "But I've gone through this before and I don't want to get hurt again." She laid a hand on his arm. "You understand, don't you?"

He nodded. "This is one of the reasons I wanted to talk it over with you first. I know what a terrible time you had getting over losing the Penner girls and Kent and Jill. It's just not fair to you to subject you to it again."

Kay did not reply immediately, but when she did there was a different tone in her voice. "If they would only let us have the triplets legally," she said, "so we wouldn't have to be afraid of losing them again–."

Danny got to his feet and crossed the room, standing before the window. "Maybe they would," he said.

"Do you think there's a chance of it?" she asked, her eyes brightening suddenly.

"Carmen seems determined to leave the triplets here and convinced that Clarence will not accept them back into their home under any consideration." He paused for a moment or two. "We can talk to her and see what she has to say."

"If they would do that I–I'd be willing–" Kay checked herself. "Danny, that's terribly selfish of me, isn't it?"

His gaze met hers. "Why do you say that?"

"The triplets need a home desperately. If we don't take them, they'll have to go to an institution. And that wouldn't be good at all, as long as we could take them into our home." New resolve rang in her voice. "I can't force them into an institution that may or may not be good for them just because I don't want to be hurt myself."

Danny shook his head in wonderment. "You mean you want to take them, anyway?" he echoed. "Even if the Ropers won't let us have legal custody of them?"

She nodded, tears glistening in her eyes. "We can't do anything else, Danny. We can't let them go into a children's home."

For a minute or two Danny remained motionless, breathing heavily. Then he started for the door.

"Are you going to talk to Carmen?" she asked.

"I thought I would."

"I'll go along."

Danny hesitated. "If you don't mind, Kay, I–I'd rather talk to her alone – at least for a few minutes."

Kay stared at him. This was the first time that she could remember he had ever wanted to keep anything from her. At first, she was disturbed by it, but she sat back in the chair, waiting. She knew that Danny would tell her what had taken place when he was ready for her to know.

Danny knocked on Carmen's door and she came to open it. Her eyes revealed that she had been crying again.

"Could you come into my study for a few minutes, Carmen?" he asked gently. "I'd like to talk to you."

"You have decided?" she wanted to know.

He nodded but did not speak aloud until they were in the study and had closed the door.

"I wanted to talk with you without Kay present," he said, "at least for now. I thought perhaps I would be able to speak a bit more frankly."

"You have decided?" she repeated once she had taken a chair.

"Yes." He sat down across from her. "We have decided."

Carmen leaned forward tensely. "You will take them, no?"

"We will take them, but only on one condition."

Her cheeks paled. "And what is that?"

Briefly he explained about the other children they had taken during the time they had been married, and how brokenhearted Kay had been when they had to leave.

"Now, Kay is willing to take them without any guarantee that you and Clarence won't want them back in a year or two. But I can't let her do it." His voice was firm and resolute. "I can't have her run the risk of being hurt so deeply again."

Carmen could not understand. "What do you mean?" she asked.

Danny spoke quietly, but there was no missing the fact that his mind was made up. "I mean that we'll take them on one condition," he said.

"And–this–this condition? What is it?"

"We will take the triplets into our home and raise them as we would our own children, on the condition that we be permitted to adopt them legally."

Carmen paused, turning the matter over in her mind.

"What does that mean?" she asked.

"If you and Clarence will sign them over to us so we have complete and permanent custody of them, we will take them into our home and make them our own children. We won't expect you to pay anything for their care. Neither would we honor a request for them to go back to Texas to live with you."

"You mean if Clarence changed his mind, they–they couldn't come back to the ranch to live?"

"That's exactly right." Danny carefully spelled it out. "We will take them, but only on the condition that they won't be taken away from us."

"But they–" her voice broke. "They are my sister's children. They should be living with me."

"I know exactly how you feel about this, Carmen," he said. "I know how hard it is for you. But I can't subject Kay to the heartbreak of again losing children who have become a part of her. If they stay with us, they'll have to stay legally and permanently."

Softly their guest began to cry. Danny waited for a minute or two before continuing. "You can think about it for a day or two, if you wish," Danny told her. "In fact, I'd suggest that you get in touch with Clarence. We don't want to press you into doing something you may not want to do."

"I understand." She smiled through her tears and, standing, she held out her hand. "Thank you, Danny. I–I want to think about it for a little while. Maybe I will call Clarence tomorrow and see if he might be persuaded to change his mind."

"You do that." He smiled. "And we'll be praying about it too. We don't want to take the children from you if there is any way for you to keep them."

When Danny went back to the living room Kay was waiting. "What did you tell Carmen?" she asked quietly. "Did you tell her that we'll take them?"

He nodded. "Under certain conditions. Carmen is going to think about it."

"Think about it?" she echoed. "What do you mean by that?"

Briefly he repeated his conversation with the triplets' aunt. Kay did not agree with Danny and told him so.

"We could take them the same as we took the others," she said. "If–if they have to leave God will give me the grace and the strength to take it."

"We can take them that way," he said. "That's true. But for some reason I don't feel that we should." He put his arm about her. "In the first place I can't run the risk of having you hurt again."

"That's no reason for depriving the triplets of a good home," she murmured.

"In the second place," he continued, "if we make a demand like this, Clarence Roper might think seriously about what he's doing. He might change his mind and let them go back home with Carmen. And, after all, that's where they belong if he'll take them."

There was a long, painful silence.

"I'm sure you're right, Danny," she answered. "All the time you were talking to Carmen I was praying that God would lead you."

"I'm positive that this is the best way to settle this."

"Only it seems so harsh – so unchristian."

"I wouldn't say that." He put his hand under her chin and lifted it to kiss her tenderly. "We've asked God's guidance. Let's leave it at that."

Although Danny and Kay got up at their usual time the next morning, when they came out into the living room they saw that Carmen had already gotten up, dressed, and had left the house. It was some two hours later before she came back. Danny heard her on the front steps and went to open the door.

"Good morning, Carmen," he said, smiling warmly. "You must have gotten up early this morning."

She nodded without speaking. Her face was drawn and dark shadows under her eyes made them seem even more somber than usual. She pushed past

Danny and crossed the room to an easy chair where she sat down.

"I called Clarence," she said, her voice wooden.

"Yes?"

By this time Kay had entered the living room and was standing near the sofa, listening.

"He–he said that he didn't *ever* want to see the triplets again."

Her eyes filled with tears.

"I'm sorry things worked out this way, Carmen."

Carmen had trouble forcing out the words. "He–he said for me n-not to come home if–if you don't take them. He said that I can't bring them back to the ranch, even to stay overnight."

Kay put her arm about the distraught woman's quivering shoulders. "I'm sure he was just angry," she said. "He couldn't feel so bitter about children. Clarence isn't that kind of a man."

Carmen swallowed. "That's what I thought before, but now I–I don't know. You've never seen such a change come over a man. He's not like he used to be at all since–since Phil said he has become a Christian. He acts as though he's wild!"

Danny and Kay both nodded to indicate that they understood what she was talking about.

"And what have you decided to do?" the missionary pilot asked.

Her gaze met his. "What else can I do?" Desperation glinted in her eyes. "I want to take Rosalita's children into our home and raise them, but I love my husband and my own children. And—and Clarence will *never* change his mind. I know that now. I've got to leave the triplets with you!"

With that she began to sob uncontrollably.

* * *

While Kay tried to comfort Carmen, Danny phoned the attorney who handled the legal matters for the mission and went down to see him. Mr. Corwin listened to the story from the beginning, making notes and asking questions.

"It seems strange that the Ropers would change their minds about taking the children," he said, "after they petitioned the court for them."

"That's what Kay and I thought. If it was up to Carmen, she would keep them. She's anxious to do so, but she says her husband has an obsession about getting the triplets out of his home. He told her this morning that she can't bring them back to the ranch. He doesn't even want her around until she's gotten rid of them."

Mr. Corwin nodded thoughtfully. "I'll get in touch with the judge who handled the matter originally, Danny," the attorney went on, "and explain the situation to him. There'll be some papers for you and the Ropers to sign and there'll have to be a hearing."

Danny took a pencil from his pocket and fingered it.

"Do you think there are any problems that could block our getting custody of them, Mr. Corwin?" he asked.

The attorney shook his head. "Not if both Mr. and Mrs. Roper are willing to sign the papers. The judge is going to want to know that the triplets are being well taken care of and will be provided a good home, but we won't have any trouble giving him references that will satisfy him on that score. As far as I am able to determine, it is just going to be a matter of going through legal channels necessary to change the custody of the triplets from Clarence and Carmen Roper to you and Kay."

* * *

All through the time of discussion with Carmen, neither Danny nor Kay had thought to say anything to the triplets, to find out what they thought about coming back to Fairview to live. When Danny got back to the house, however, Doug and Del were sitting on the porch, waiting for him.

"Hi, guys," he managed a bright smile.

They only frowned at him.

"Now, what's the matter with you two?" he wanted to know. "You look as though you've lost your best friend."

It was soon apparent that the boys were not in a mood to joke. They studied Danny seriously, but it was some time before either of them spoke.

"We've been wanting to talk to you, Danny," Doug finally said.

"OK." Danny sat down on the steps and turned to face them. "What is it that you've got in mind?"

It was all the boy could do to force out the words. "Is–is it true that Uncle Clarence won't let us stay at the ranch anymore?" he demanded.

"Who told you that?" Danny parried. Somehow, he had never thought that there would be any question in the minds of DeeDee and her brothers about coming to live with him and Kay. The adults involved had taken it for granted.

"We came into the house a little while ago," Del put in, "and Aunt Carmen was sitting in the living room bawling like everything. She didn't know we were around, and we heard her say that she was afraid she would never get to see us again."

"And," Doug added, "we figured maybe they–they weren't going to let us stay with them anymore."

Danny looked from one to the other but did not speak.

"Uncle Clarence was awful mad at all three of us before we left," Doug went on. "You should've heard him."

"It isn't because he doesn't like you," Danny explained. "It's the gospel that he objects to."

The boys nodded. "We know that."

"He got mad when we led Phil to Christ," Del continued.

"That's what your Aunt Carmen said. She told Kay and me that he got so angry he said he was going to put the three of you into a childcare institution of some sort, somewhere in Texas."

Their eyes widened, and their concern gave way to fear. "You aren't going to let him do that, are you, Danny?" they asked.

The missionary pilot shook his head. "Of course not. And your aunt doesn't want to have you in a children's home either. That's the reason she brought you up here to stay with Kay and me."

The boys stared at him momentarily, as though they could scarcely believe what Danny had just said.

"You–you mean you and Kay are planning on letting us stay with you? We can stay here in Fairview and not have to go to a–an institution?"

"That's right. That is, if you want to."

"If we want to?" Doug echoed. "That sounds wonderful!"

"We're as happy about it as you seem to be," Danny told them.

"Happy about it?" Del echoed. "It's going to be a lot better than going to an old orphanage." He turned to his brother. "See, I told you that Danny and Kay wouldn't let them do anything like that to us."

He quickly got to his feet. "I'm going to find DeeDee and tell her the good news."

There was a short silence after Del left. Danny saw that the lights in Doug's usually merry eyes had died, leaving them dull and expressionless.

"What's the matter, Doug?" he asked quietly. "Don't you like the idea of staying with Kay and me?"

The boy looked up. "Sure I do," he said lamely. "It's going to be great staying here with you and Kay, only–." His voice trailed off.

"Only, what?"

A wistful tone crept into his young voice. "Only it sure was a lot of fun being down on the ranch. They've got horses to ride and everything." He paused momentarily. "Why, we even had our own saddle horses. We got to take care of them ourselves and help with the work around the ranch and everything."

"I'll bet that was great," Danny replied, taking a deep breath. "You know, when I was a boy, I went out to Colorado to school and once in a while we went horseback riding. We used to have great times."

Doug brightened just talking about it. "I got so I could ride my horse bareback on a fast gallop," he said. Thinking about the saddle horse he would have to leave on the ranch caused the lights to die in his eyes once more. "Uncle Clarence said we were coming so good with our riding that it wouldn't be long until he'd teach us how to rope calves. Then we–we had to leave. Now I don't suppose I'll ever get a chance to learn."

"I don't think I'd go as far as to say that," Danny told him.

"But you don't have any horses or calves."

"That's right," Danny said, "I don't. But I wasn't thinking about that. I was thinking about the Circle R."

"But Aunt Carmen says that Uncle Clarence will never let us go back there. She says–."

"I know what she says, and I'm sure that at the moment that's exactly the way the situation is. But it's only because your uncle is so bitter against God. We should pray that he'll make a decision for Christ the same as Phil did. Then he'll want the three of you to come down to the ranch to visit."

"Do you think *he* could ever be reached for Christ?" Doug asked, as though that was too great a miracle to think about.

"Sometimes when people are so bitter against God, it is because they are afraid to know the truth. Perhaps God's voice is already talking to your Uncle Clarence. Yes, Doug, I think we definitely should pray that he'll come to Christ."

Doug's eyes lit. "If that happened, he would let us come back to the ranch and visit, wouldn't he?"

Danny nodded.

"Maybe he'd even let us go back there and stay again," Doug continued.

The boy's simple statement chilled Danny. This was something he hadn't counted on. He had just assumed that the triplets would want to stay at Fairview with him and Kay. He had never before considered the fact that they might prefer to stay on the ranch in Texas.

CHAPTER 9

STARTING SCHOOL

Tearfully Carmen Roper left Fairview on the Twin Cities' bus the day after Danny went to the attorney and started action on the adoption papers. Kay suggested that she and Danny take Carmen back to Minneapolis to catch her plane, but their guest insisted on going alone.

"Thank you so much," she said, her voice taut and strained, "but I–I think it will be easier this way. I–I have to think."

Danny and Kay nodded understandingly.

"Just as you like," Danny replied, "but we would be glad to take you to the airport."

She shook her head. "No, this is best. Besides, you have already done so much for us. I don't know what I would do if it weren't for you. I would have had to see the triplets go into a children's home. I don't think I could have stood that."

Danny followed her outside and talked to her while she waited for her cab to take her to the bus depot.

"If you change your mind, Carmen," he said, "just let us know before the papers are signed and we'll stop the action at once. The triplets are your sister's children and both Kay and I recognize that you have the first right to them if you want to exercise it."

Tears flooded her dark eyes. "No," she retorted, "it is not my right to have them. I have had to make a choice." She choked for a moment and could not go on. "You will take Rosalita's children and raise them in peace and harmony. With Clarence so-so–." She tried but could not find the words to express herself. "It would only be fighting and discord to have them stay with us on the ranch. It is better that they are with you."

"If you're sure that's what you want," Danny repeated, "it's fine with us."

"I didn't sleep much last night," she said, "but as I lay awake, I decided that this is the way it should be. It is best for Doug and Del and DeeDee."

Relief flooded over Danny. This was what both he and Kay wanted. The house had been so empty with only the two of them and Jim. And now Jim would be going away to Bible school, and they would be alone. It would be good to hear laughter and excited young voices in the house again.

"We'll take as good care of them as we know how, Carmen," he assured her. "They will be *our* children."

"That I know." She seemed almost happy as she

smiled. "Last night I got to thinking about Rosalita and Jerry. I know I am her sister, and from that standpoint she would want me to have the children, but when I think about the religion that meant so much to both of them, I think maybe Rosalita would rather have the triplets with you."

At first Danny did not understand what she was talking about. "What makes you say that?" he asked.

"You will raise them as she and Jerry would have raised them, had they lived," Carmen continued. "They will have the same training they would have given them – the same example in your home." Her voice was hushed. "I don't know that I understand it, but I got to thinking that maybe this is God's way of answering their prayers for the triplets."

The cab pulled up to the curb. While the driver waited impatiently Carmen kissed the triplets good-bye, tears streaming down her cheeks. DeeDee and Del and Doug stood beside Danny, watching until her taxi rounded the curve and went out of sight.

"I wish she didn't have to go," DeeDee observed, tears glistening in her young eyes. "I wish she could have stayed here."

"So do I," Doug answered, sinking his teeth into his lower lip. "Do you suppose we'll ever get to see her or Phil or Marie again?"

"Of course you will," Danny broke in, speaking confidently. He knew it would take a minor miracle in their Uncle Clarence's life before that was possible, but he didn't believe that Carmen could manage to stay away from the triplets when she knew where they were, even if she didn't have legal custody of them.

"What I'm wondering," Doug said, "is whether we'll ever get to see the ranch again. I'm sure going to miss living down there."

"Me too," his brother added.

Kay, who had been watching in silence from the porch, came out to join them. "Why don't you all come into the kitchen with me?" she asked brightly. "I believe I just happen to have the makings for some hot chocolate, if there's anyone here who would like to have some."

Doug shook his head. "I don't believe I feel like eating anything right now, Kay."

"Neither do I," Del added.

Danny eyed his wife significantly. "I believe I'll go down and fill the car with gas," he told her. "Want to come along?"

She hesitated. "Do you think the kids will be all right?"

"Oh, sure," Doug said. "You go ahead. We'll be OK."

They left the triplets alone in the front yard and went to the car.

"I don't like the idea of leaving them," she said when they had pulled away from the house and were moving down the street. "They seemed so sad."

"I think it was best for them to be alone for a little while. They may want to talk to each other and say some things they wouldn't care to have us hear."

Kay glanced over her shoulder at the forlorn trio. "Do you think they'll want to live with us?" she asked with growing uneasiness.

"I was beginning to wonder about the same thing," he answered. "They certainly are upset."

Kay nodded. "I feel so sorry for them, Danny. I'm sure they feel terribly alone right now."

"I'm sure you're right about that. Carmen is their closest living relative, and right now they don't know whether they'll ever see her again or not. It's a big blow to them."

"Being driven out of the Roper house hasn't helped any either. They must find that awfully difficult to understand. When Rosalita and Jerry were alive and someone they had prayed for had received salvation, the family would have been overjoyed. It must be bewildering to them to have Clarence get so mad over it."

They pulled into the station and Danny asked the attendant to fill his car with gas and check the oil. Once they were alone again, he glanced at Kay.

"We're going to have to have a lot of patience with them," he told her. "This is probably almost as difficult for them as the death of their parents."

They drove by a discount store window filled with school supplies.

"That window display reminds me of something," Kay put in, changing the subject. "We're going to have to see that the kids are in school."

"I hadn't thought of that. Should we enroll them this afternoon?"

Kay frowned. "I don't know, but I would just as soon wait until tomorrow morning. They're so upset right now, I don't like to have to make them go to school today. Perhaps they'll be feeling better in the morning."

"OK." He sighed his resignation. "They can wait until tomorrow, but they should go then. It will be easier for them once they get started and have to study. They'll be kept so busy for a while they won't have time to feel bad."

Silence hung between them.

"I feel terrible for Carmen," Kay finally said, "but I can't help being elated, too. It's going to be so wonderful having kids in the house again. Right now, I can scarcely believe that it's true."

Danny did not answer her. He was thinking of the expression on Doug's face as he spoke so longingly about the ranch. It would be good for him and Kay to have the triplets, that was true. But how would the kids feel about it? That was the thing that mattered the most right now. If they were miserable staying in Fairview, that would be no good, regardless of how glad he and Kay were to have them. They would have to make it a matter of prayer.

When they drove back to the house the triplets were glumly sitting on the front steps. Danny started out to them but changed his mind and turned back. There were times when a person would rather be alone. And for the triplets, this was one of those times.

The following morning Kay got the triplets up shortly after seven. Doug came out of the bedroom he shared with Del, carrying his shoes and rubbing the sleep from his eyes.

"Why are we getting up so early?" he wanted to know. "We didn't have to get up this early at Uncle Clarence's unless we wanted to."

DeeDee answered him. "Don't you know? We've got to start school today. Or haven't you thought of that, silly?"

He scowled at her. "Start school?" he echoed. "You've got to be kidding."

"No, I'm not. If you don't believe it, just ask Kay. She'll tell you."

Doug hurried to the kitchen and questioned Kay.

"That's right. We want you to start school this morning."

"Now, that's a happy thought."

Kay ignored his disapproval. "Danny is going to take you to school and see that you get everything taken care of."

Doug bristled. "We can take care of ourselves. We don't have to have anyone go along with us to help us get started."

"I think it's better if I go with you this once," Danny said. "There will probably be some questions the principal will want me to answer."

Del, who had come into the kitchen just then, turned to Danny. "What's this about?"

"I was just breaking the sad news to Doug and DeeDee you have to start school today."

"Start school?" His young face crinkled. "Can't we finish this year by correspondence, as long as we got started that way?"

Danny laughed pleasantly. "I'm afraid the school authorities would take a very dim view of that, Del," he said. "And even if they didn't, I believe I'd insist on it."

The boy's frown deepened. "You sure do treat your kids mean," he muttered jokingly. "That's all I can say."

Danny caught the banter in his tone. "I'm treating you the very same way that I got treated when I was your age, Del. I want you to know that you're no better than I was."

"When I get married and have kids my age, I'll let them study by correspondence. I won't be mean to them."

"We'll see about that."

Kay broke in. "We'd better get to the table and have breakfast," she said. "If we don't, there won't be time for devotions this morning."

They glumly went to the table. Nobody talked much during breakfast. When the time came for prayer and Danny asked for requests, DeeDee suggested that they pray for their Aunt Carmen.

"I felt so sorry for her," she said. "She didn't think I noticed it, but she was crying when she left here yesterday."

Del nodded. "And I think we should pray for Marie and Phil too. And especially for Phil. I can tell you right now, it's going to be rough on him living with Uncle Clarence now that Phil's a Christian."

"We should pray for Uncle Clarence," Doug said. "He's really a nice guy when you get to know him. He gave us our own horses and everything. I don't think he wants to be mean to anybody. Right now, he's just mad at the gospel and doesn't want any of his family to have anything to do with it."

"I'm sure that what Doug says about Uncle Clarence is right," Danny observed. "I've seen guys like him who were so determined to have nothing to do with Christ that they'd fight against Christ and anyone who was a Christian."

Danny glanced at Kay. "Why don't you start by praying for Uncle Clarence, Kay?"

When the prayer session was finished, Kay got her jacket. "Well, it's time to go to school. Are you ready, kids?"

"As ready as we'll ever be."

Del hung back. "Do we have to go now, Danny?" he asked. "Can't we put this off until tomorrow?"

Doug spoke up quickly. "It's like getting a tooth pulled. If we've got to do it, we'd just as well get it over with."

Danny and Kay took them to the office of the grade school principal halfway across town. Miss Kirby met them solemnly, with no sign of friendliness, and sat down to look over the records Danny and Kay had brought with them. The boys glanced at one another with growing uneasiness. They had never gone to a real school before; this was a new experience. And they weren't entirely sure they were going to like it.

Only DeeDee seemed excited about the prospect of going to a regular school. She sat there, bright-eyed and eager, clinging to every word the principal said.

Doug and Del saw her enthusiasm and could scarcely hide their disgust. Imagine! Having to go to a place like this and being happy about it.

From time-to-time Miss Kirby paused to look over the papers, tapping them thoughtfully with her pencil.

"Hmm."

"I hope these are all the records you will need," Danny said. "They're all the children brought with them, and there's no way of getting any more."

"They will do." She shuffled through them once more. "However, it would have been much better if they could have started with the rest of us the first of the school year. They are going to start at a little disadvantage." She paused. "But I suppose we'll have to make the best of a difficult situation."

Doug and Del studied her sharp features obliquely. Already they had decided that they didn't think they were going to get along too well with her. She got to her feet, and for the first time, they learned that she could smile.

"If you'll come with me, I'll take you to your class and introduce you to your teacher."

Danny and Kay went one direction and the triplets went the other, following Miss Kirby down the long hall to the sixth-grade room.

"Miss Leslie," the principal said, "I'd like to have you meet the Davis triplets, Dorothy, Douglas, and Delbert. They'll be in your class."

"I'm so glad to have you." Her smile was genuine. The boys decided right away that she was going to be easier to get along with than the principal.

Miss Kirby left them with their new teacher. When she was gone Miss Leslie turned to them, smiling warmly.

"You can take desks at the end of the last row," she said, "but first I'd like to have you meet the rest of the class."

Every eye in the sixth-grade room was focused curiously on them.

"Class, these are the Davis triplets. They're going to be with us now. Won't that be nice?"

Smiles welcomed them.

She put a hand on DeeDee's shoulder. "This is Dorothy. Is that what you're called at home, my dear?"

DeeDee shook her head, the color creeping into her cheeks as she realized she was the focal point of attention. "They call me DeeDee."

"If you'd like, we can call you DeeDee too."

She nodded gratefully.

Miss Leslie glanced at the boys and paused; no doubt disturbed by the fact that they looked so much alike.

"Let's see," she began. "I believe I've forgotten your names."

Doug spoke first. "I'm Del."

"No, I'm Del."

The class snickered, and Miss Leslie eyed them helplessly.

"You both can't be named Del."

"I was just teasing you," Doug said. "My name's Doug."

This time it was his brother's turn. "No, my name's Doug."

Again, the class snickered.

"Which of you is Doug and which of you is Del?" Miss Leslie demanded, looking from one to the other.

"We change names every once in a while," Del told her.

The teacher rapped for order, but Del continued as though he had not heard her. He hadn't had so much fun since they used to fool the visitors who came to visit their mission station.

"Yeah," he said, "that's the way it is. My name's Doug in the morning and Del in the afternoon."

"No, I'm Doug in the morning. You're Doug in the afternoon."

"That's the way it was last week."

By this time, the entire classroom was in an uproar.

"Class! Class! I must have your attention." Miss Leslie stood and pounded the desk with a tiny fist. Finally, the class quieted until she could make herself heard. "We've had all of this foolishness that we're going to have." She turned sternly to the boys who were standing beside her. "If we have any more of this nonsense, I'm going to send you both to Miss Kirby's office."

Reluctantly Del and Doug went to their seats.

It was not long after they got home that afternoon that Danny came back from the airport.

"Well," he said, "how'd school go today?"

"Not bad."

They both grinned at him.

"Y'know, Danny," Del said. "I think school's going to be all right, after all."

THE DANNY ORLIS SERIES

The Danny Orlis series, by Bernard Palmer, delivers a blend of adventure, mystery, and suspense through various settings—from the Canadian wilderness to Guatemalan jungles. Danny Orlis, an adept outdoorsman, skilled athlete, and committed Christian, employs his quick thinking, calm bravery, and biblical solutions to confront everyday problems and hair-raising dangers. Early stories focus on Danny navigating school life, sports, and outdoor challenges, while in later books, Danny and his wife Kay provide wisdom and guidance to youngsters facing lifelike situations and challenges. Having sold over two million copies, this series has made Palmer a renowned author in Christian youth literature. Palmer is also the author of the Felicia Cartright series and various other series for Christian youth.

AVAILABLE FROM WWW.ANEKOPRESS.COM

www.ingramcontent.com/pod-product-compliance
Lightning Source LLC
Chambersburg PA
CBHW060503300726
48975CB00008B/2628